MAP *of* PLAGUES

A MAPWALKER NOVEL

J.F. PENN

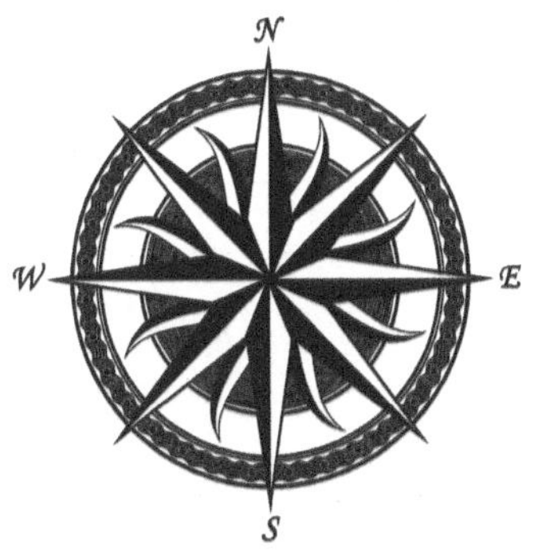

Map of Plagues. A Mapwalker Novel Book 2
Copyright © J.F.Penn (2019). All rights reserved.

www.JFPenn.com

ISBN: 978-1-912105-36-6

Requests to publish work from this book should be sent to:
joanna@CurlUpPress.com

Cover and Interior Design: JD Smith Design
Printed by Lightning Source UK

www.CurlUpPress.com

"We are a plague on the Earth."

David Attenborough

"Anyone who was alive during the outbreak
of the bubonic plague in the 14th century experienced
something terrifyingly close to the widespread
death and chaos of an apocalyptic event."

Alan Huffman, International Business Times

PROLOGUE

THE STORM BROKE OVER London in the early hours
of the morning. Rain crashed down onto the cobbled street
that ran past Traitor's Gate, the passage to death in the Tower
above. Lightning flashed, forking across the city, illuminat-
ing the skyscrapers that reached heavenward. A confident
city, secure in its power, with no heed of the threat below.

Beneath the gate, the murky river Thames began to boil.
A fetid stench bubbled from the depths as four men swam up
from below. As they reached for the shore, another flash of
lightning caught their faces in profile. Hard ridges of bone,
thick jaws set in determination and the half-moon tattoo of
the Warlord that painted their faces in shadow.

As the Feral Borderlanders climbed from the water,
pulling their muscled bodies easily up the side of the wall, a
man stepped from the shelter of the Tower. He wore a plague
doctor's mask, the hooked beak of an ibis, the Egyptian bird
of the dead. Two bags lay at his feet.

He called softly down to the climbing men. "Quickly
now. We don't have much time."

The four men changed into dry clothes, pulling up hoods
to hide their faces in this city of ever-present cameras. Two
hefted the bags onto their backs. The plague doctor pulled
a long cloak around him, set his face against the storm and

led the men around the perimeter of the Tower. He glanced up at the symbol of a once-great empire. Fragile flesh would rot away but these stones would remain even as a new power took this city in the days to come.

The men crossed Smithfield within sight of what had once been the Royal Mint, the white imperial facade of what was now the Chinese Embassy lit with spotlights from below. They skirted the edge of the light, staying in the shadows, until they reached a door on the building beyond marked with No Entry signs. It was bolted and padlocked, set with multiple alarms. The plague doctor stood in front of the door and the four men ranged around him, alert for danger.

A spark of flame from his fingers, a flash of electrics. The bolts fell off, the padlock dropped, the door clicked. He held his breath for a moment, half expecting the high-pitched squeal of alarms. But it remained silent.

The plague doctor pushed the door open and the men stepped inside. They turned on torches, revealing stone steps that wound down into darkness. Water dripped from their clothes onto the stone, droplets as dark as blood. It smelled of damp earth and decay.

They headed down with heavy footsteps, their boots marking time like the inevitable march of history.

At the bottom, they emerged into a wide cavern, the roof supported by metal reinforcing pillars so as not to disturb the graves beneath. The excavation was just one of many in London, part of the ever-expanding development of the transport network. This site had once been a Cistercian Abbey and in 1349, during the Black Death, it had become a plague cemetery, a mass grave for the diseased bodies of parishioners.

Pieces of rope bisected the site, dividing the plot into specific areas and orange flags marked the bodies beneath. Skeletons embedded in the dirt reached for freedom, bony fingers clutching at the air as if they tried to rise again even as their remains crumbled to dust.

The plague doctor ignored these common dead, his cloak swirling about him as he strode to the back of the cavern where a stone wall barred the way. It was made from mismatched blocks, some of the stones weathered as if they had once stood against ferocious storms like the one raging outside. The plague doctor ran his fingertips over the blocks, leaning close to them as if he could sense their history through his skin.

According to ancient texts, these stones had been carried from Jerusalem, taken from the rubble of the Second Temple, borne across plague-ravaged Europe to stand guard at the entrance to the knights' final resting place.

After years of research, the plague doctor suspected that the graves of those who fought the plague also rested here. A secret order of knights who believed that the contagion ravaging the continent had been sent by the Devil himself, a curse that could somehow be lifted by those of faith — and power. Secret annals suggested that they had achieved their goal, pushing the last of the plague out of this world — and into another.

But after years of searching in the Borderlands, the plague island was still out of his reach, lost as the borders continued to morph over time until the original contours disappeared. The only chance to find it now was the map that the knights had made, a map of skin made from plague victims that linked to the island of the dead, a portal back from that lost world to this one.

The plague doctor thought of the gleaming skyscrapers in the city above, the millions who slept secure in their beds. They had no idea what was coming for them.

He stood back from the wall. "Take it down."

The four men with half-moon tattoos put down the bags and pulled out lump hammers, shovels and picks. One man hefted the weight of a hammer, a grin spreading across his face as his meaty hands dwarfed the handle.

He stepped toward the wall and smashed the weapon into the stone. The sound echoed through the chamber but the blow made scarcely a dent. The man swung again. Another stepped beside him and together they pounded the ancient wall, muscles flexing.

The striking of metal on stone rang through the plague pit but the plague doctor was confident that the thick walls of the old Cistercian Abbey would shield the noise from above. By the time the workers arrived in the morning, his team would be long gone.

The men hammered away until they made a hole in the wall big enough to step through, then stepped back, panting with exertion. Sweat ran down their faces, carving a path through the dust that had settled on their skin. The plague doctor held his torch high and stepped through the hole into the chamber beyond.

The mass grave of the outer room was crammed full of the dead, but this inner tomb was spacious. Intricately carved arches rose to a dome overhead painted with faded images of demons devouring plague victims beneath the watchful eye of a vengeful god. Around the walls, deep niches held the remains of the band of brothers, but the plague doctor ignored them and stalked toward the centerpiece of the vault.

A huge stone sarcophagus sat in pride of place in the middle of the chamber topped with the effigy of the knight who slept beneath. He lay resplendent in full armor, the pommel of a longsword clutched between his hands. Lichen covered his craggy face, eating away at the features of a man who had been feared once, but was now forgotten in time. The plague doctor pointed, his finger shaking just a little as he considered what might be inside.

"Open it."

Two of the men hefted the lid from the top of the stone sarcophagus, grunting with effort as they pushed it to one side revealing darkness within. The smell of rotted leather with a metallic edge filled the air, permeating even the plague doctor's mask as the men pushed again. The stone crashed to the floor.

The plague doctor walked to the edge of the sarcophagus and peered in. A suit of armor lay with its hands on its chest, sunken in death, the patina of age turning the once shiny metal to rust red. A yellowed skull grimaced from within the helmet, bones held together by metal hundreds of years after death. This knight had died fighting a foe that could not be beaten by any sword, a creeping invisible enemy that slaughtered loved ones with no hope of reprieve. The plague doctor could only imagine what this man had done to try and rid Europe of the devastation.

In his skeletal hand, the knight clutched a rough box fashioned from lead with rivets at the edges. The plague doctor reached for it, his heart pounding. He had searched for so long, could this finally be the moment?

As he touched the knight's hands, the bones turned to dust, leaving the box resting on top of the armor. He lifted it from the remains and beckoned for light. One of the men shone a torch at the box while the plague doctor gently levered the top open.

A folded piece of parchment lay inside, grimy with the dust of generations but still intact. The plague doctor lifted the tattered piece of parchment from its resting place with care, placing it lightly on the stone beneath. He unfurled it, revealing a piece of an ancient map, the edges rough where it had been ripped into quarters. It was only one fragment, but it was the beginning of the end for Earthside.

"The plague wreaked havoc on Europe," he whispered. "Some say it killed six in every ten people. It heralded the end of civilization." He looked more closely at the tattered map, a silver-grey gleam in his eyes, like a wolf identifying its prey. "It can do so once again."

CHAPTER 1

MORNING SUN LANCED THROUGH the windows of the flat above the old map shop, lighting on the walnut wood bookshelves laden with notebooks and leather-bound journals. The cry of seagulls wafted in as they hung on the breeze above the Georgian streets of Bath, tasting the ocean on the air as it blew inland from the Bristol Channel.

Sienna Farren sat cross-legged on a cushion by the bookshelves, a tendril of titian hair escaping from her blue striped headscarf as she pulled down another of her grandfather's journals. The cover was grey leather, faded in parts, marked by the sun of another time. It looked like elephant skin, but as she ran her fingers over the whorls and lines, she sensed a different vibration. It was from a creature of the Borderlands, lost to Earthside but hunted over there, brought back in death.

The journals captured fleeting moments from the years that Michael Farren had spent as a Mapwalker on missions off the edge of the map. That world was lost in time, but the moments he had spent watching were captured here on the page, passed from his memory to hers across the generations. Sienna had not really known her grandfather in the years before he was murdered, sacrificing himself to save the city of Bath from Borderland invasion. She had inherited his map shop as well as his lifelong mission and in many ways, she was still trying to come to terms with the new direction of her life. These journals were an insight into the mind of a man she wished she had known better in life, but perhaps could still help her even in death.

She flicked through the pages of the journal, past line drawings in thick black ink, some highlighted with color. A bright kingfisher sketched on the edge of a sparkling stream with feathers of burnt orange and turquoise, his spiked beak slightly open. A mountain range with numbered passes, a thin line to show the path of the Mapwalker team. Red-hot lava spilling over the top of a volcanic cone, trailing a path of destruction toward a village that lay beneath.

The face of a young Nubian woman gazed out from another page, loving lines and delicate shading betraying a deeper connection. Sienna wondered who the woman was, and how long ago her grandfather had loved her.

She read on past pages of temples and buildings and ruins, some overrun with vines, others as pristine as if they had been built yesterday. He had noted the sounds and smells of the jungle next to the sketches, the call of monkeys, the fecund aroma of tropical flowers. The scent of berries rose from the page, the purple ink made from the juice of some unusual Borderland fruit that Sienna didn't recognize.

The journals were numbered with tiny Roman numerals etched into the spine. They were ordered on the shelves, but number twenty-four was missing. Her grandfather's compass was still missing too, stolen by a Shadow Cartographer just round the corner from the map shop where she now sat. Sienna wondered where the notebook was now.

She understood that the sketchbooks weren't absolute truth, they were her grandfather's perception of a moment of time. But who's to say where art, truth and history intersected? The notes he made and the drawings he sketched told his version of the tale, even if the annals of the Mapwalkers told something different. None of those who traveled there could take pictures. The boundaries of the Borderlands turned all technology to dead metal. When the borders were formed in the days of stronger blood magic, only the old ways remained off the edge of the map. So Michael had used pen and ink, paint when he could. Charcoal, ash, dust.

Blood.

Sienna pulled up her shirt sleeve to reveal her healing scars, tattooed ley lines of The Circus and the Royal Crescent. Her grandfather's skin had the same lines, his own blood map providing protection for the city of Bath and the portal that they guarded here. Now it was Sienna's turn to be the guardian of the gate. But she wanted more than that. She wanted to be fighting the Shadow Cartographers, trying to build a future for the Borderlanders.

Alongside Finn.

She flicked through more of the pages, pulling down the journals faster now. Her grandfather had traveled all over the Borderlands. He must have visited the trader town on the edge of the Uncharted, he must have known a way to get back there. Sienna thought of Finn's face as he stepped back through the gate as the border closed around him. It had only been a month ago, but it felt like forever. He had said his mother came from the slave markets there and after the battle with his warlord father, it made sense that he would flee to the edge of Borderlander civilization, where there were plenty of places to hide.

But it was hard to find and she couldn't just walk back there through a map of her own creation. She had no context, no anchor, and as with all locations in the Borderlands, its position changed as new places were pushed off the edge of Earthside. As the landscape of the Borderlands shifted, it pushed the trader town even further into the Uncharted. Few dared stay too long, as time moved differently out there.

Sienna wondered if Finn thought of her. She saw his face

every night when she closed her eyes, and she longed to go to him.

But there was also a darker thread to her desire.

When she had cut into her skin and used her blood to create a powerful map, she had let the shadow inside. Now it beat within her, drawing her back to the dark magic of the Borderlands, pulsing deep within her heart.

She had to go back there, but she didn't want to go alone. There was one person who understood this craving, one person she could trust. Sienna picked up her phone and texted Mila.

* * *

The low thrum of the engine beat time as the canal boat moved slowly through the water under the shade of overhanging trees. As her phone buzzed, Mila Wendell kept one hand on the tiller while she read the text from Sienna.

When are you back?

A bark of excitement made Mila look up as Zippy, her golden cocker spaniel, greeted the local ducks as they turned toward the aqueduct at Dundas, just a few miles out from Bath. Sunlight dappled the water with shades of green and the smell of elderflower rose from the hedgerows as they passed.

After the battle with the Borderlanders, Mila had fled the city, needing time to let her body return to its Earthside physicality. She could travel in the ripples between waves, spin liquid into weapons, turn her body to water. It was freedom, but every time the Mapwalkers used their magic, a sliver of shadow weaved its way inside — and Mila knew that she had used too much of it in those last days.

And yet every day for the last month, she had fought the desire to go back to the Borderlands alone. She held Zippy close in the night, weeping into his fur as she resisted the pull to darkness. It was an addiction that only grew worse with time. Their mentor, Bridget, had warned of this and it was why Mapwalkers must always travel in teams into the Borderlands. If they had too much shadow, they could no longer cross over for fear of losing themselves. Too many of their kind had been lost over the years, too many had shifted into Shadow Cartography.

Like Xander had done on the last mission.

Once the golden child of Mapwalker lineage, his skill as an Illustrator had marked him out for greatness, but he had betrayed them all for a chance to use his magic every day. To stop resisting the dark.

Mila understood why he had made that choice, but she hoped that she could resist it long enough to help Sienna find Finn and maybe, just maybe, there was a chance for peace between Earthside and the Borderlands.

Zippy ran up and down the roof of the canal boat, happiness on his doggy face. He knew the smells of this place, and they both had friends here, friends who would look after the little spaniel when she had to travel alone. It was time to moor up again, to settle for a time in a place she had come to call home.

Mila texted back. *Soon.*

* * *

In the stone corridors beneath Bath Abbey, the whoosh of fire echoed before ending in a metallic slam. The sounds repeated again and again, faster now, until suddenly it stopped. Peregrine Mercator leaned over, hands on his knees, panting with effort, his t-shirt damp with sweat in the over-heated room.

As his breath slowed, Perry stood again and pulled the

human-shaped target back toward him across the wide expanse of the practice room. It was made of thick metal, but its heart had burned clean through with his repeated attack. Perry nodded, pleased at his improved precision. He was not the same man who had faced his father a month ago. He was stronger now, his muscles more defined, his magic under control.

He sent the target back once again, opened his palms and conjured the fire once more. While the other Mapwalkers had to be careful of using their magic on Earthside, he was a Halbrasse, a half-breed, able to move between the realms, born with shadow already in his veins, choosing to stay and fight for the world he had grown up in. This was his home and when they came for it again, he would be ready.

He slammed flame into the head of the metal target once more, seeing his father's face melt away with every blow.

* * *

Outside the door of the training room, John Farren sighed as he watched Perry's anger explode. He leaned heavily on his cane, the barely healed scars on his back preventing him from standing upright, part of his mind still chained in the bloody dungeon of the Borderlands. He understood the depth of the young man's pain, and he saw a reckoning ahead with the man who had wounded them both so deeply. Sir Douglas Mercator, Perry's father — and the Shadow Cartographer who had tried to make a blood map from John's own skin.

An alarm sounded suddenly, a deep note of warning.

John turned from the window and limped away down the corridor. In years past, the sound had been unusual but these days, it seemed the borders were tested several times a day, the Borderlanders pushing against the limits of their world, finding ways back into Earthside. For generations, the magic of the border had been taken for granted, but now it seemed, it was beginning to crumble. It was only a matter of time before they faced a proper invasion and this world would have to face a truth hidden for too long.

He reached the War Room. Bridget Ronan stood before a computer screen showing a map of the south of England, a red light pulsing above the City of London. A deep frown creased her beautiful face, and as she leaned to look more closely, her multi-colored patchwork dress swirled around her legs. As it shifted, John remembered one night when they had danced together under the full moon on a ruined terrace above a forgotten river deep within the Borderlands. The scent of spring blossom hung in the balmy air and the sound of the water splashing below drowned their cries of pleasure as they lost themselves in one another. That night they had left their responsibilities behind, a stolen moment off the edge of the map. But they had returned to real life soon after, the memories fading as he returned to his Earthside family, and she took on a different role in the Ministry. It had been their last mission together.

Bridget looked up, her expression softening as she saw him standing there. Perhaps the memories hadn't faded after all. Perhaps there was still a chance for them. But with the amount of shadow now within him, John knew he could never go into the Borderlands again. He was stuck on Earthside, as Bridget was too, both of them tainted by the magic they had used on the other side of the map.

Bridget turned back to the screen and zoomed in on the map to show a plague pit behind the City of London.

"A small group of Ferals breached one of the secondary gates under the Thames. It seems they only had one goal." She pulled up pictures of a tomb surrounded by security tape, then a sarcophagus, an empty box upon the remains of a knight. Above it, the painting of a demon devouring plague victims as the dead piled up in mounds around it. She clicked through to security footage of a man in a plague doctor's mask.

Bridget frowned, biting her lip in concern. "I think they found the first piece."

John reached for her hand. "It's not over, then?"

Bridget shook her head. "It's only just beginning."

CHAPTER 2

THE ROCKY BEACH WAS busy even in the small hours of the morning. Fishermen readied their boats and traders joked with one another as they warmed their hands by braziers, beacons of flame against the dark. A woman in a black headscarf squatted on her haunches on the stones in front of a fire, her hands shaping balls of dough into smooth round shapes which she threw on the coals with practiced skill. The smell of fresh flatbreads mingled with the tang of smoke and salt in the air.

Finn Page wrapped his thick cloak more tightly around himself, scant protection against the cold wind blowing in from the sea, but more as a shield against anyone recognizing him. His face was on Wanted posters all over the northern Borderland towns but down here, on the very edge of the Uncharted, he should be safe. People here tended to turn a blind eye, since many were also amongst the wanted themselves. He had escaped through the network of the Resistance, but he couldn't stay anywhere for long, not wanting to draw down the wrath of his father on those who sheltered him.

Finn leaned back against the wooden spars of the jetty, gazing toward the horizon and the faint glimmer of dawn. The sun would rise whatever happened to him. The world turned regardless of whether his life ended in the dungeons of the Shadow Cartographers.

He thought of Sienna on the other side of the map and wondered whether she thought of him at all. Time moved differently out here and the kiss they had shared as the border closed had begun to fade in his memory now. It was crazy to think that he could love an Earthsider, that they could ever find common ground. But Sienna gave him hope that things could be mended somehow, her optimism as yet unshaken by the Shadow.

A light flashed out in the gloom, a lamp held aloft by new arrivals. Another lifeboat filled with refugees rejected from Earthside. They had chosen to leave their homeland for fear of death and chaos, but they were not wanted by anyone else. As each nation turned them away, they became lost on the seas and flickered over the border. These last few months, they had arrived in their thousands, spirits broken by the journey and constant rejection from those who should have let them stay.

Finn understood the feeling of loss. Since he had stepped through the portal in Bath, turned his back on that glorious city and Sienna, he had been running from his father, the Warlord of Old Aleppo. His father threatened death for his betrayal, but more than punishment, Finn regretted the loss of his home. The sweet smell of oranges from the market as he sipped strong coffee with his friends, the stacks of his father's library filled with contraband books, walking for hours through the streets of a city he had grown up in and knew every corner of. He even missed his father's laugh as he played with his younger children. The Warlord was a pleasure-loving family man when he was not away slaughtering his enemies — and perhaps now there was hope.

In the last few days, Finn had heard through his Resistance contacts that the Warlord talked of amnesty, a willingness to trade. Finn could live safely in one of the lesser Borderland cities, his niece, Emily, would be returned to him, rescued from the Halbrasse training camps. They would be left alone to live in peace. It sounded like an impossible dream, a tranquil life where he could raise his niece in memory of her mother, Isabel. He had promised to keep Emily safe as his sister took her dying breath, but now that promise haunted him. Finn gripped his sword, knuckles white with tension. He was a warrior, always had been, always would be. While he wanted a better life for Emily than the halls of the Halbrasse, he also couldn't see himself tending orchards in the outer cities for the rest of his life.

But he had to know more about his possible future, so he was here, ready to meet with a messenger from his father. The rocky beach served well as a public place where he could slip into the shadows if it looked like a trap. The bounty on his head was still worth collecting, after all.

The sound of oars paddling grew louder than the waves as the lifeboat drew closer to the shore, hollow-cheeked men onboard still rowing with tired arms. They wore layers of stained and ragged clothes, pockets filled with what little they could carry from their homeland. Some wore hats pulled low over their eyes as if to shield the world from their sight. Finn glimpsed the drawn face of a beautiful young woman clutching a silent baby boy in her arms, her big dark eyes staring toward an unknown shore.

The traders readied themselves on the rocks, jostling for position, ready to guide the travelers to what they thought was safety.

But Finn knew what really awaited these people.

This was not the coast of some welcoming haven where refugees would be helped into a new life. This was the Borderlands, where those pushed off the edge of the map ended up in forgotten places, where history remained in the present, and the extinct lived on. It was ruled by the Shadow Cartographers, those who could wield dark magic, who bred a new generation focused on taking back the land they believed was theirs. Earthside, where Sienna lived, where a whole world of people lived their lives with no idea that the Borderlands or the Uncharted even existed.

Finn watched the new arrivals. They would learn soon enough.

The boat beached on the shore with the grating sound of metal over stone. The traders helped people out, guiding them up the bank, funneling them toward the soldiers who waited on the crest of the hill above, faces painted with the half-moon of the Shadow. The new arrivals spoke the names of their home towns, the places they had fled for fear of their lives, hoping for news of home, of family, of those who had left before them. Those on the beach merely shook their heads, denying any knowledge.

Soldiers singled out the ones who might be especially useful. One pointed at the beautiful young woman, proof of her ability to breed held in her arms. One of the traders pulled her away from the group.

She turned, calling out to an older man. "Papa!"

The man started up the beach toward his daughter. "Wait, what are you doing?"

He pulled papers from his jeans, the sodden pages almost legible. He thrust them at the soldier, but the man brushed them away, the papers fluttering to the floor. "These are worthless now."

One of the traders pulled the old man roughly back. "Leave her. She is no longer yours."

"No!" The old man struggled but more of the traders piled in, punched him to the ground, kicked him as the girl was dragged away screaming, the baby crying, the sound of lamentation in the air.

Finn closed his eyes against their suffering and clenched his fists as he tried to hold himself back. There were too many for him to fight alone and he had no friends here. The girl would probably end up in the breeding halls where his sister had died in a bloody dungeon not so long ago, buried in the mass grave behind the Castle of the Shadow. The girl's father would probably die in the mines of the Uncharted. This is what the Resistance fought against, but they needed a whole lot more help to overthrow the power of the Shadow Cartographers and he could not fight this battle alone.

As the traders stripped the boat for parts, the refugees were herded away. By the time the sun rose above the horizon, the only thing left on the beach was a child's doll, choked with seaweed, trampled into the sand.

Finn turned to see the willowy figure of a woman standing alone on the jetty, black hair loose, swirling about her in the wind like the snakes of Medusa. She carried twin crossed swords on her back and her face was marked with the half-moon. As the rays of dawn touched the jetty with a golden glow, Finn recognized her. Jari, one of the Warlord's trusted bodyguards, renowned for her skill with the sword and her brutality in battle. They had trained together in their younger days, matched in skill on the battlefield — and in their passion afterwards. She was even more beautiful now with the scars she wore with pride. Finn remembered the shape of her muscled body beneath that cloak. He could still recall the warmth of her. He shook his head. His father knew him too well.

He watched Jari from the shadows, waiting for any sense that she wasn't alone. Minutes passed and she stared resolutely out to sea, her cloak flapping in the breeze.

Finn stepped out into the open, hand on his sword, checking around him for danger.

Jari looked over. "I came alone, as promised." Her eyes flashed with a dark smile. "Besides, if I wanted to take you, I would. I hear you're out of practice, Finn."

She sat down, long legs swinging off the edge of the jetty. She seemed relaxed but Finn was still wary. She was right, he had been running and hiding for too long, and his sword arm was out of practice. Jari could probably even beat him in hand-to-hand combat, but he hoped they wouldn't have to try that right here.

"What does my father want?"

Jari paused for a moment, her dark eyes raking over his body as if she remembered those nights years ago as well as he did.

"The Shadow Cartographers seek pieces of an ancient map that show the way to an island lost in time, pushed out into the far Uncharted."

"What does that have to do with me?"

Jari raised an eyebrow. "The Warlord knows of your love for Earthsiders and they will come soon looking for your help to find the pieces of this map. We have one fragment already and they will do anything to find the rest."

Finn's heart raced at the thought of Sienna coming over the border again. He would see her once more. But he could not betray her. If the Mapwalkers needed the ancient map, then it must have power to destroy something on Earthside. He turned toward the ocean, the frown deepening between his eyes.

"I can't—"

Jari cut him off. "Your baby niece has no magic."

Finn spun back to face her. "What? How do you know? She is too young to face the test."

Jari jumped off the jetty and walked toward him, her gait swaying slightly as if she danced across the rocks. Finn grasped the pommel of his sword and she gave a half-smile at his gesture, like a cat toying with its prey.

"There is one whose magic is knowing gifts early, reading the blood of the newborns to see where their talents lie. To see who is worth keeping."

Finn flinched at the thought of little Emily's blood taken for a dark purpose.

Jari walked closer. "Do you know what they do with those who have no magic in the Castle of the Shadow?"

Her words were soft, menacing.

Finn closed his eyes, recalling the thick stone walls of the dungeon, the bodies of the dead, the Blood Gallery, the torture chambers — and the mass graves of those considered worthless to the cause.

He sighed and nodded slowly.

Jari put her hand on his arm and looked up at him with a half-smile on her lips. "She is safe, looked after by the wet nurses, kept from the blood pits — for now. She'll be returned to your care if you bring the three missing pieces of the Map of Plagues to your father in Old Aleppo by the end of the next half-moon. You can raise her in peace, your transgressions forgiven." She shrugged. "Who knows, maybe Kosai will want to play happy families. After all, she is his granddaughter."

Finn spun round, shaking off her hand, his face contorted with anger. "That bastard sent his own daughter to the Castle of the Shadow. Do you know what happens to women in those breeding halls? Women like you?"

Jari laughed in his face. "Not like me. Your sister was weak, easily broken. The question is whether you are, too."

She was so close that Finn could smell the mint tea on her breath, see the pores of her skin, sense the latent strength of her body. How he wished to fight her now, see her proud face in the dust, but what she offered would fulfill the vow he had made to Isabel as she lay in a pool of her own blood. He promised to look after Emily and he could not storm the castle by force. He had tried before and been vanquished by mere children trying out their newfound magic.

Finn stepped back, giving ground before meeting her eyes. "If I do this, then I want safe passage for the Mapwalker team. I will find the pieces of the map but they must be allowed to return to Earthside afterwards."

Jari hesitated a moment, then nodded. "The Shadow Cartographers want the Map of Plagues, not the people you have a fondness for. Their fate is sealed, regardless, like all those on Earthside."

Finn could only hope that her words were empty, that there would be a way to prevent disaster, but for now, he had to move toward saving Emily. He would figure out the rest later, with Sienna by his side.

"Then I'll do it."

Jari smiled again. "There is just one more condition."

CHAPTER 3

Sienna turned the sign on the door of the shop to Closed. The maps behind her rustled, their pages calling to her as portals to adventure, or a warning of places lost in time. She hadn't even been through the entire inventory yet, the wonders that her grandfather had preserved in a lifetime of cartographical collecting. Each map was potential in paper form, a way into another world, and Sienna longed to place her fingertips on the ink and step through, no matter the price she would have to pay.

She sighed and stepped outside, locking the door with her grandfather's key. Sienna still thought of it as his even though he had left everything to her, along with the legacy of protecting the city he had loved all his life. Now it seemed it was threatened once again. Bridget's voice had sounded tense on the phone as she summoned the Mapwalker team to the Ministry.

As Sienna walked along, the bright sun lit up the pedestrianized street of Elizabeth Buildings, colorful with flowering window boxes. The smell of freshly roasted coffee filled the air from the cafe across the way. It was difficult to imagine that these streets had run with blood not long ago as feral wolves ran through the gate followed by the Warlord's soldiers threatening far worse. They had been vanquished that day, but they still strained at the gates between the worlds.

Sienna turned onto Brock Street, the giant plane trees of The Circus looming ahead. When all was well in the city, red double-decker buses cruised these streets filled with eager tourists listening to the glittering history of the Roman spa and Georgian elite. The buttery Bath stone glowed in the sun, and for the first time, Sienna considered that this could be her home. Her grandfather had loved Bath so deeply that he had given his life to save the city. She had never formed that kind of attachment before, but perhaps now, it might be possible.

Thoughts of Finn intruded. She had promised to help him bring down the dark regime of the Shadow Cartographers, to free the children and enslaved women. That world seemed so far away from this perfection of a city where life was easy and free.

Sienna walked down through the busy streets, past the independent shops, packed restaurants, and the faces of happy families with no idea of that other place.

She turned into the paved square of the Abbey Churchyard and looked up at the facade of the great church, the vaulted stained glass windows flanked by Jacob's ladder carved in stone on which angels climbed heavenwards. Her eyes were drawn to the sinister angel that crawled down, its contorted body more like a demon. Most never noticed the anomaly, but then most didn't know of what lay below this ancient place. The winding halls of the Ministry of Maps lay buffered up against Roman ruins, wound amongst the remains of an ancient city, powered by the ley lines that the Druids of old had known so well.

Sienna walked around the back of the Abbey to the doorway she had run from the first time she had been confronted with the truth of the Mapwalkers. Now she entered again willingly, hoping that this was her way back to Finn.

"Wait for me!"

Sienna turned to see Mila in the alley, walking toward her with confident strides. Her dark curls were tied back with a red scarf patterned with grinning sugar skulls that matched her goth t-shirt, pulled tight over lithe curves and the web of tattoos on her arms.

Sienna smiled. "I'm so glad you're back. I've been going nuts here without you. How was your escape?"

Mila shook her head. "Not long enough. What's going on?"

Sienna shrugged. "Not sure. But Bridget said it was urgent."

Together they walked down the steps and entered the corridors of the Ministry. They passed doorways for the main departments: Antiquities, Restoration, Misinformation, Illustration. The Blood Gallery.

Sienna clenched her fists as they passed, a cord of emotion pulling her toward what would one day be her own resting place. As a Blood Mapwalker, the most powerful magic flowed through her family line, and one day she would have to pay the ultimate sacrifice.

By the time they reached the War Room, it was busy with Mapwalker staff talking in smaller groups, gathered around a framed image of giant rats devouring a corpse.

Bridget raised her arms and calm descended on the room. She nodded to the screen behind her. "Last night, a tomb was uncovered behind a plague pit in London." The screen flicked to images of a sarcophagus, the stone lid broken next to it, then a group of men, one wearing a plague doctor's mask, four with half-moon tattoos.

"These men broke in and we believe they found something, something we thought lost many generations ago."

The image on the screen changed to a woodblock carving, hard black lines revealing a grim tableau. A man lay dying, his face contorted with pain, bulbous black growths under his arms. Rats gathered under his bed, his family gathered behind him, and beyond them, a hooded figure stood with a scythe.

Bridget closed her eyes for a second, as if gathering strength, then opened them again, the brilliant blue as hard as sapphires. "We don't have any pictures of the Map of Plagues, but we think a part of it was found last night by these men."

Questions came thick and fast across the room, the noise growing louder until Bridget held up her hand for quiet. "I'll tell you all we know from the histories. As the Black Plague ravaged Europe, a group of Mapwalker knights tried to save what was left by opening a portal and pushing the badly infected onto a forgotten island in the Borderlands, effectively quarantining them from Earthside."

Perry frowned. "And damning those on the other side. They're people too, you know."

Bridget nodded. "We can't escape the sins of the past, but regardless of what was right, that's what they did. After they pushed the final plague villages into the Borderlands, they used the skin of victims to create a map marking the resting place of the cursed island. The Map of Plagues."

As Bridget spoke, Sienna touched the scars on her arm, her own skin an evolving map of Bath. Had those men been distant relations of her own blood? She felt her father's eyes upon her, and she turned to smile at him. His face was old beyond his years now, marked by the passage of time he had spent as a tortured prisoner of the Shadow Cartographers. She had barely recognized him when they found his carved up body shackled to a table and Sienna knew his scars ran deeper than the wounds that scarred his flesh.

Her father's blue eyes were filled with concern, his knuckles white around his cane with worry, but he wouldn't hold her back from this mission. He had spent years protecting her from the secret of their bloodline but now she was here, now she had taken her place on the Mapwalker team, she knew he was proud of her.

Mila pointed at the woodcut of the plague victim on the screen. "Can a medieval plague really have an impact on the world these days?"

Bridget tapped on her tablet computer to bring up recent news reports of a plague outbreak. Health workers in white plastic clothing and face masks tended to living victims while the dead lay in body bags in neat rows waiting for cremation.

"It's not medieval. The plague still emerges every year in Madagascar, and has been present in Congo, and even the western states of America."

Perry stepped forward. "Don't we have vaccines or ways to stop it?"

"There is no vaccination for bubonic plague but it can be treated with antibiotics, so it's controllable. The problem comes when the plague goes pneumonic and becomes airborne, spreading through coughing and contact." She paused, her frown deepening. "We think the Shadow Cartographers will use the Map of Plagues to find the most virulent strain, the one that the knights banished over the border, and then somehow send it back over to Earthside. Coordinated attacks have been increasing. They're testing our defenses."

Bridget pointed at the map again as the red dots of plague overran the stricken continent, leaving millions dead. "This is what the Shadow Cartographers mean to bring back. We can't let it happen. We have to find the Map of Plagues before they do and destroy it."

"Where do we start?" Mila asked. "Are there any clues in the archives?"

Bridget shook her head. "The knights didn't trust anyone, even their own kind. They split the map into four pieces and separated them. There have been fragments supposedly sighted over the years, notes in the annals but nothing concrete." She hesitated. "There is someone who might know more but she is deep in the Uncharted."

John stepped forward, shaking his head. "You can't send them there, Bridget. It's too dangerous. The Librarian hasn't been seen since …" His voice trailed off.

"Since the last time we sought her out," Bridget finished for him, and a moment of understanding passed between them. "Time passes differently out there. She may yet help us again."

Perry walked up to the screen and examined the plague doctor. He zoomed in and tapped on the man's face. "I can't be sure but I think this is my father's work. He won't stop until Earthside is destroyed and the Borderlanders retake what they think is theirs." He spun around, face set in determination. "When do we leave?"

Bridget frowned. "You need a guide to the outer Borderlands and possibly even into the Uncharted. The trader town on its northern edge is the best option. We've found many guides there over the years, people willing to risk traveling with us. It has no name so it cannot be found easily and its position shifts, of course, but there is one way you can get there quickly. Follow me."

Sienna's heart beat faster at the mention of the trader town. Could it be the same place Finn had run to? As she followed the others toward the door, her father stopped her with a gentle hand.

"Be careful," he said softly. "I know how the shadow feels." His eyes were haunted, like an addict remembering the early days before magic ravaged his body. He shook his head. "I'm sorry, I should have prepared you—"

"It's okay, Dad. I'll be fine. We can talk when I come home again."

He nodded and waved her on with a smile. "Go then. Be safe with your friends."

The others were way up the corridor now, waiting outside a locked door, one of the many hidden beneath the ancient city. Sienna hadn't noticed this one before. It was nothing special, just a wooden door, stained and varnished to enhance the natural grain. But as she drew closer, Sienna noted the intricate locking mechanism that held it shut. Carved runes surrounded a silver keyhole and she could sense magic wound within, as if it would only open to those chosen for a purpose.

Bridget pulled a silver key from her pocket and placed it within the lock, whispering words under her breath as she turned it. She pushed open the door, her blue eyes sparkling with a love for adventure. "Welcome to the Gallery of Geographical Maps."

Sienna couldn't help but gasp as Bridget turned the lights on overhead. The gallery stretched ahead of her, the length of a football field, with bright colors of earth and sea on either side and above her, a vaulted ceiling of gold extravagance.

Each painted map was as big as the wall, a bird's-eye view of a region of the world, shaded with detail of the land. Olive groves and mountains, white-capped sea and calm turquoise lakes. Walled cities of grandeur, rural villages and sea ports with ships that headed out into the blue. A tingling in her fingers made Sienna lean in more closely to one of the cities. She sensed that she could use these to travel through, a shorthand version of the more detailed maps held within the vaults, or those she could make herself. This was some kind of Mapwalker portal room, with access to places the team had traveled to in the past — and perhaps had still to visit.

Bridget led them down the gallery and stopped in front of a fresco of Italy. "The way that leads to the trader town is hidden in the map of Rome itself." She traced the lines of the city with a gentle fingertip. "See, this quarter is not of the ancient city on Earthside. You can enter through here."

Sienna reached out a hand and caressed the lines as she imagined diving down into those streets. Would Finn be there?

Bridget stepped back to allow Mila and Perry to stand close to Sienna. "Be careful out there, but remember, we need those pieces of the Map of Plagues, whatever it takes."

Sienna sensed the pull of the Borderlands and as it pulsed through her, she closed her eyes. She held out her other hand to Perry and Mila and as they touched her palm, she led them through the map.

* * *

The energy in the room shifted as the team passed through. The wall of maps seemed to ripple in their wake and Bridget put out a hand to catch the air that passed through. Was that the salt of the ocean she could smell? The smoke from cooking fires?

She remembered traveling to the trader town years ago, the thrill of being on the edge of adventure as her team passed through on their way to the Uncharted. Bridget sighed. She could never walk there again. She could never swim in the forgotten lakes of sparkling emerald or walk in the hanging gardens. She could never again visit the lost cities of legend. She could not feel the dark thrill of shadow in her veins, the intensity of the rush that came from crossing over.

She wrapped her arms around herself, clutching her body tightly, holding herself back. Because of course, she *could* travel again. She was a Blood Mapwalker, all she had to do was walk through the map.

But Bridget could barely contain the throb of shadow as it called to its home. Every time she had used her magic, the darkness burrowed deeper within her, its tendrils wrapped round her heart. She could cross over again but one more drop might be enough to tip her over. She thought of Sir Douglas Mercator, Perry's father, once her colleague — once her friend — fighting alongside the Mapwalker team to maintain the border in times gone by.

Until the drops of shadow grew too strong in him, and he turned.

Bridget took a step closer to the detailed map, her fingers tracing the lines that represented the border. Would this desire remain in her for the rest of her life? Would she have to resist it every single day?

She rested her forehead against the wall, closed her eyes, allowed the need to rise up within her. She could leave, forget all that held her here, forget John and her responsibilities, forget the fight over the border. It would be simpler to just let go. The tug of shadow throbbed within her and Bridget let it rise …

She stepped back from the wall quickly, heart hammering as she realized how close she had come.

She took a deep breath.

She could not give in. She could never use her blood magic ever again, for it would cost her everything.

CHAPTER 4

THE CASTLE SMELLED OF damp and decay and Xander could never quite get his clothes completely dry. He huddled on his bed, pulled the blankets tighter about his shoulders and leaned back against the wooden headboard, carved with intricate designs of poisonous plants. Mold grew in the corners of his room and despite covering the flagstones with thick rugs, it was always cold. There was a fireplace surrounded by fancy metal scrollwork but nothing to burn and no way to start the flame anyway.

Xander sighed. This was *not* what he had signed up for.

His access to the hidden libraries had been refused until he could prove himself a true follower of the Shadow. He didn't have any friends because the castle was full of guards below his station and feral children with no control over their magic. He had tried to get into their hall but the little freaks had driven him away with fireballs and cruel laughter. He was allowed — even encouraged — to visit the Fertility Halls but the place made his skin crawl. He was truly an outsider here.

When Sir Douglas Mercator had first talked of the glories of the shadow side, he had spoken of unlimited magic, of a forbidden library full of books of beasts that Xander could illustrate and skin maps he could use to conjure them into being. He promised a fulfilling life in the Borderlands, the life of a prince, no longer subject to the demands of the Ministry, no need to restrict his magic. All he had to do was deliver the daughter of John Farren, so her skin alongside her father's would complete the Map of Shadows, and Xander would have his new life.

He had fulfilled his promise and brought Sienna to the castle but somehow, the Mapwalker team had made it out. Xander still remembered her face as he had revealed his true allegiance, how Perry had lost his father that day and how he had lost his friends.

He'd also lost his prize and so Xander found himself consigned to the castle, living not the princely life he'd been promised, but a limbo existence unwanted by all. Sir Douglas hadn't mentioned the bleak living conditions here in the castle or that the forbidden library would still be forbidden, or that the skin maps he had been promised were kept locked up to be used for more important things than conjuring beasts.

On top of all that, Xander had been without his phone for missions into the Borderlands but he had never really considered a life without technology altogether. It pretty much sucked.

Despite his annoyance at Bridget and the Ministry and the dire warnings of what would happen if they gave in to the shadow side, he found himself missing Bath. The way the stone turned to honey-gold in the late afternoons, the birdsong along the canal where he had walked with Mila sometimes, Zippy her spaniel running ahead. Right now he even missed Perry. He could start a fire anywhere and right now, the warmth of the flames would go a long way to making this place bearable. Xander wasn't even getting a chance to use his magic, since Sir Douglas was holed up in his study at the top of the north tower and hadn't been seen for days.

Enough.

Xander unwrapped himself from the blanket and grabbed the satchel containing his sketchbook and pens. He would just go knock on the door and ask — no, demand — access to the forbidden library. That would be a start until there was something more interesting to do. Like summon the cool beasts he'd soon be drawing. After all, what was the point of being an Illustrator when you couldn't illustrate? He would prove himself to the Shadow if it took all his magic to get there.

* * *

Xander stalked through the corridors of the castle, the stone tunnels lit with lamps in iron brackets, the cold permeating his bones. He passed soldiers along the way, some staring at him with searching eyes, assessing his status. He met their gaze, noting their features, determined to seek them out once he was given his rightful place here. They would respect him when they faced the creatures he conjured.

As their footsteps faded into the distance, Xander reached the bottom of the staircase to the north tower. It was flanked by two pillars carved with occult symbols on one side and the crest of the Mercators' on the other. Xander put his foot on the first step, hesitating as the cold seemed to permeate deep into his blood, filling his veins with ice. He looked up, a sudden doubt filling him. What was really up there?

Perhaps he should come back another time? Perhaps Sir Douglas was too busy to see him right now?

Footsteps echoed behind him as the soldiers marched back down the corridor.

Xander walked on, taking the steps two at a time, unwilling to face them as he retreated. His heart pounded as he climbed, the welcome exertion of physical movement combined with one concern.

He had not been invited.

Xander slowed his steps to stop on the curve of the stair and pulled a scrap of leather from his pocket. Placing it on the ground, he smoothed out the edges around the beasts drawn there: a tentacled sea monster and a shark in one corner, a dragon in the opposite, next to a coiled serpent and a powerful lion.

Xander summoned his Illustrator magic and channeled it into the leather. Asada, the lion, stepped from the map, shaking his thick golden mane as if waking from sleep. He rolled his powerful shoulders and nuzzled against Xander's side, his purr a deep sound that echoed in the corridor. Xander put his face in Asada's mane, closed his eyes and breathed in the animal scent mingled with the leather of the map. This was about as close to home as he could get and for now, it was enough. With Asada by his side, Xander's confidence returned. Together they padded quietly up the stairs.

As the staircase spiraled up into the upper reaches of the tower, Xander looked out of the slits in the rock which opened to the castle and lands below. On one side, guards trained in the quadrangle in front of huge double doors leading to the children's wing. On another, a group of women in rags stood around a pile of bloody shrouds, those who didn't make it out of the Breeding Halls alive. Carrion birds swooped low over the burial pit, their cries a haunting ululation to honor the silence of the suffering victims. Xander looked away and redoubled his pace, Asada at his heel.

As they reached the top of the tower, Xander slowed, taking quiet steps toward the giant wooden door which stood open a fraction. He could hear voices from further inside, although they were faint. Sir Douglas had a whole suite of rooms up here in the tower, so Xander pushed the first door open with a gentle hand and stepped inside.

The plush apartment was cosy, warm with a crackling

log fire and animal skins on the walls for insulation. Xander reached for Asada's mane as he noticed a lion pelt next to a rare leopardskin. Life was cheap here, even more so for animals.

Sir Douglas's wide mahogany desk dominated the space, a map of the Borderlands placed on top, the corners weighed down with the tiny skulls of children.

Xander started as the voices rose in argument, now clearly coming from the next room. He knew that he should leave now but something about the map drew him in.

The Ministry had many maps of the Borderlands but all were of different parts and they shifted over time. As new places were pushed over the border, the very shape of the Borderlands changed as it squashed some cities closer, pulled apart mountain ranges, and nudged rivers off course.

But this map was a recent survey, a bird's-eye view of the whole expanse all the way to the Uncharted with the addition of tent cities that Xander had never seen before, each drawn close to portals that he definitely did know about. The biggest tent city near the shadow gate that led into Bath through the portal at The Circus — right in the heart of the city he had left behind.

As Asada lay down by the fire, licking his paws and enjoying its warmth, Xander walked around the other side of the desk. Rounding the corner, his foot knocked against something leaning on the side. A plague doctor's mask with a long beak once stuffed full of medicinal herbs. Xander frowned at the curious thing. He wasn't aware of Sir Douglas's interest in medieval times, but then there was a lot he didn't know about this side of the border.

The argument grew louder still on the other side of the door, and Sir Douglas's voice became clear.

"The plague could spread further than we can control. It's too dangerous. Our people—"

His words turned into a scream, an agonizing sound of terror and pain.

Asada stood, hackles raised, and bared his teeth as the scream trailed off. Xander clutched the table, eyes wide as he stood looking at the door. He wanted to go in there, he wanted to help, but something stopped him, something cold and dark that pierced his heart with a lance of shadow. He didn't want to face what lay behind that door.

A broken voice stuttered, faint through the door, "I'm sorry, my lord. Please …"

The scream came again.

Xander fled, Asada on his heels as they ran for the safety of the lower halls.

Even as he reached his room and barred the door, Xander knew that something had sensed his presence, something knew what he had seen and heard, something was out there waiting for him.

He sat on the floor, his back against the wooden door. He put his arms around Asada's neck and buried his face in the lion's mane once more. Tears welled in his eyes as he wished he could take back the decisions he'd made. How had he ended up here? Was there any way he could fix this terrible mistake?

CHAPTER 5

SIENNA LEANED INTO THE sense of weightlessness as she flew above a world that shifted along an ever-changing boundary. The lines of the walled map morphed into three-dimensional streets next to an ocean that stretched into the distance. The world curved into the horizon and for a moment, she couldn't tell whether she was in the map or above it. Could she keep traveling up here, far beyond the border?

She swallowed the exhilaration and dived down into the city, giddy with sensation.

The smell of rotting fish and the salty tang of the ocean greeted Sienna as she opened her eyes. They were in a street behind a food market, the shouts of stallholders blending with the call of seabirds above them as they dived down to snatch pieces of discarded produce. Sienna could just make out the ocean beyond the maze of stalls, the clean blue a stark contrast to the riot of color and movement within the market.

Perry crouched on the ground retching.

"I don't know if I'll ever get used to that," he groaned.

Mila pulled him up by one arm. "Come on, we have to get moving. The Shadow guards will sense the breach in the border and we don't want to be here if they come looking."

They skirted the edge of the market and headed into the warren of dirt streets that led away from the waterfront. They were dense with makeshift shelters, shacks made of rusted iron sheets tied together with rope leaning up against each other and hung with plastic tarpaulin to keep out the rain. Some were sturdy, reinforced with planks of wood and metal rivets, others cobbled together with flotsam from the ocean.

An old woman sat on a low plastic chair smoking a hand-rolled cigarette, the sweet smell of smoke hanging in the air around her, disguising the stink of the open sewer nearby. She watched them pass with glassy eyes, no trace of curiosity left in her.

A chicken strutted past, pecking at the dust. Dried fish hung in strips from one shelter, pungent with salt. A make-shift kite of rags flew high above, a glimpse of red against the blue, a sign that perhaps there was still some hope here.

"I've heard that this place has no name because no one stays long enough to call it home," Perry said as they walked on. "Thousands of people pass through but none stay to build anything."

Mila walked faster. "Well, we're not staying long either."

They passed people of all cultures along the way. Veiled women of Middle Eastern origin, Africans in bright colored headpieces, and men with the tall blonde features of Slavs.

"How do all these people get here?" Sienna asked.

"If they're lost on water, they end up here," Mila said. "The lucky ones might find a place to call home."

Sienna frowned. "And the unlucky ones?"

Shouting and the sound of drums came from the streets ahead. People on the streets faded quickly into the shadows, alert to danger.

Mila looked ahead, her eyes narrowing. "The unlucky ones find out this is a slave trader town."

They headed in the direction of the drums, harsh beats

that reverberated in the narrow lanes, and soon joined a throng of people heading in the same direction. There were merchants in the crowd, and soldiers too, those who could use slaves perhaps, as well as those in need of entertainment.

The Mapwalker team kept their heads down, merging with the pack as the streets opened out into a large square. The smell of roasting nuts and hot sugar filled the air, and a folk band played in the corner, the atmosphere almost like a carnival as the late afternoon sun lit the square with a golden glow. Sienna looked around at the excitement on the faces around her. Humanity had ever loved to watch a spectacle of suffering.

A raised dais stood in the middle of the square covered in colored streamers, a long metal cage in its center. Soldiers of the Shadow stood around it, their posture relaxed but alert and ready to act should the crowd surge forward. Sienna rose up on her tiptoes to see better. A chill washed over her as she saw what lay within.

The cage contained seven people, five adults and two children, faces desperate as they clutched at the bars. From their clothes, they had only recently crossed from Earthside, refugees lost on the ocean or perhaps they had wandered over the border during some desperate situation. War drove people over here, escaping from one life only to enter another just as dangerous.

The crowd cheered as a muscled hulk of a man stood up on the stage, a wooden cosh in one hand. The weapon was dented and stained with blood and sweat. The slave trader had the ruddy face of someone who enjoyed life too much but the cruel look in his eyes made it clear that his enjoyment involved the suffering of others.

"Are you ready?" he called across the heads of the crowd.

The baying of voices rose to the sky as the mob clamored for spectacle and drama, a moment of escape from their own pitiful lives. Sienna tried to crush down the nausea that rose within as the slave trader pulled a young boy from the cage, his meaty hand wrapped around the scrawny wrist of a nine-year-old with the olive skin of the Mediterranean and the dark eyes of Hispanic descent.

"This one is something special. Found him myself in the camps lighting fires with his magic." He shook the boy. "Show them."

The boy cowered away from the man as tears ran down his cheeks, his face frozen in fear. The slave master pushed the boy to the ground and raised the wooden cosh, ready to strike. "Show them, boy!"

Sienna couldn't bear to watch any longer. She took a step forward, raising her arm in a bid to catch the attention of the slave master.

A strong hand pushed her arm back down, holding her wrist in a tight grip.

She spun around. "What are you …?"

Her words trailed off as she looked up into the face of the man who stood behind her. Dark eyes and the regal features of an African prince.

Finn.

He pulled her away, shielding her body with his own as he led her out of the central area to the edge of the market.

"Are you trying to get yourself captured?" he demanded as soon as they were out of sight of the slave master. He shook his head in frustration. "This place is crawling with Shadow guards and spies who will betray you for a loaf of bread."

She looked up at him, heart thumping. "Hi."

Finn took a deep breath. His eyes softened and he lifted a hand to stroke her cheek. "Hi." He shook his head. "I'm sorry. I saw you there and I couldn't let you draw attention to yourself."

"But those people—"

"You can't help them. You saw the soldiers guarding

them, the crowd waiting to see them fall. It's the same as the Castle of the Shadow. We couldn't save all those women in the breeding halls, we couldn't save the children either." Finn hung his head. "I don't know who we can save anymore."

Sienna reached up and cupped his face in her hand. "I missed you."

"I missed you too." Finn wrapped his arms around her, pulling her close so their hearts beat together. He bent his head to kiss her, his lips just touching hers.

"Don't mind me."

Finn pulled back at the mocking voice, leaving Sienna bereft. She opened her eyes to see a willowy woman with black hair tied back with a leather strap, twin crossed-swords on her back. Scars snaked up her lean muscled arms and her face was marked with the half-moon tattoo of the Warlord. Her tawny eyes raked over Sienna.

"This is the one you turned your back on your family for?" The woman raised an eyebrow. "She must be good."

Sienna blushed.

Finn cleared his throat. "Sienna, this is Jari. We're … working together at the moment."

Mila and Perry pushed through the crowd, emerging at the edge just in time to hear Finn's words. Jari took a step back, hands hovering near her swords now she was outnumbered.

Mila glanced over at her then directed her question at Finn. "We need a guide to the library and we need to go tonight. We don't have much time. You know of anyone who might be able to help?"

Finn hesitated and Sienna thought she saw a flicker of uncertainty cross his face, as if he had to make a choice in that moment. She desperately wanted him to say he would come but what did she know of his life now — and who was this Jari, with her stark beauty that was so intimidating?

Jari stepped forward, hands resting by her side now, a

half-smile on her face. "We're free, actually, and we were just talking about a possible journey. It's been a while since we've traveled together, isn't it, Finn?"

Sienna heard a possessive edge in her words, a hint of an intimate history that made her burn inside.

Finn took a deep breath. "What do you need?"

Mila explained a little about the Map of Plagues. "We need to get to the Library of Alexandria, or what's left of it."

Jari laughed. "When you push places out of Earthside, they thrive here. You destroy and write them off your maps, but here, they live again. The library is far greater than it once was. And it's not too far from here — *if* you know the mountain passes."

Her words hung in the air.

Mila looked directly at Finn. "We only need one guide."

Finn glanced over at Jari and a look passed between them. He sighed. "We travel together. It's both of us, or none at all."

Sienna sensed that there was something going on, something that trapped Finn into this arrangement somehow. She could only hope that he would tell her at some point, but for now, they needed to get moving and she didn't want to leave him behind.

"We don't have much time," Sienna said, putting her hand on Mila's arm. "And we do need a guide."

Mila bit her lip, narrowing her eyes at the warrior woman. "I don't like it. Even our friends have betrayed us before."

Jari shrugged. "Your loss." She began to walk away.

Finn took a step back, his eyes darting between Jari and the Mapwalker team. "I … have to go with her."

Mila put a hand out. "Wait. If you vouch for her, Finn, then we'll accept the terms."

Jari stopped and turned back. A beat of silence before Finn spoke. "We have fought beside each other in many battles. Jari will keep her side of the bargain, as I will keep mine."

Sienna couldn't help feeling that his words had a deeper level of meaning and there was a sadness beneath his tone that she couldn't quite put her finger on. But at least now they would have time together and she could find out what was going on.

Mila nodded. "Alright, let's get moving before night falls." Her eyes didn't leave Jari's back as the warrior woman led them out of town in the gathering dark.

They soon passed a queue of ragged people lining up for a soup kitchen. There were splashes of color but most were dressed in the brown and green and grey of dirt and mud and broken earth. The smell of roasted vegetables filled the air, the promise of a full belly drawing people here from all over the makeshift city.

A young woman, belly swollen with late pregnancy, leaned against the wall. She smoked a hand-rolled cigarette and as they walked by, Sienna caught the almost sweet smell of marijuana but with a taint of something else underneath.

Finn noticed her confusion. "People will do anything to escape for a while, but the drugs here are often laced with other things — experimental compounds aimed at mutation."

Sienna shook her head in horror. "Why would anyone do such a thing?"

"Mapwalkers are born, not made, you know that as well as I do. The Shadow Cartographers seek new strains of magic and they don't have any restraints on how that's achieved."

Mila joined in the conversation. "Unlike on Earthside where the Mapwalkers are dying out."

"Because we don't force people to breed like they do here," Sienna snapped, remembering the Fertility Halls of the Castle of the Shadow.

Finn's jaw tightened. "Your people on Earthside are not at war. At least they don't know they are yet, but over here, the drums beat harder every day for invasion, and wars need people to fight them."

As they walked on, his words echoed in Sienna's mind. Back in Bath, it was hard to imagine what war might look like, how Earthside could be changed by invaders from the Borderlands, but Finn was right. Mapwalkers dwindled on Earthside, but here they bred new blood every day and each birth was a chance that more powerful magic would emerge. Even if they found and destroyed the Map of Plagues now, what did it all mean for the future? She had promised Finn she would help him fight for peace between their worlds, but suddenly that seemed so far out of reach.

The densely packed makeshift housing grew more sparse as the team walked south, past the edge of the shanty town as it spilled into the desert. The night air smelled fresh out here and Sienna took some huge breaths, suddenly aware that she had been shallow breathing in the city to avoid inhaling the stench.

The cry of a night bird called from above, the silhouette of a raptor hovering overhead. Sienna shuddered to think of it swooping down to pick at the carcasses of the dead from the city behind them.

Undulating dunes rose as they walked toward a distant ridge far ahead, the rising moonlight casting a silver glint on its slopes where a path wound up into darkness.

As Finn led them out into the desert, they saw a column of refugees heading over the hill in the opposite direction. Families huddled together carrying what they could, bent shoulders, slow steps.

"Where are they going?" Sienna asked.

Mila glanced back at them. "I heard talk in the market of a refugee camp in that direction, a place where the sick are cared for, with enough food and even protection from slave traders."

Jari gave a harsh laugh and shook her head. "This is the Borderlands. You think there'd be something like that here? I don't know what's out there but there's no way it's some paradise. Those people are marked by the shadow. They have no future."

The warrior woman strode ahead, her words leaving the team in silence as they walked into the night.

At the edge of the desert, just before the land rose sharply into the escarpment, a ruined temple rose out of the valley floor.

"We'll stop there briefly before we journey on," Finn said.

They reached it as the moon rose high above the ruined temple, casting a silver light upon the statuesque figures of long-dead gods.

Finn knelt by the altar, his dark head bent in respect, his lips moving in silent prayer. His fingers caressed the pommel of his sword, held in front of him like a rosary.

Sienna watched him from the side of the ruined temple. She had never had a faith like his, perhaps she never had cause to. Faith helped in the darkest of times and even when her father had gone missing years ago, she had relied on books and learning, rather than God to answer her questions. Of course, the holy books on Earthside had no light to cast on the split world. There was no place for Borderlanders in their singular history.

She wondered how the priests and shamans here explained the split. Perhaps she could study their holy books and find out. Perhaps that way she might understand more of Finn's world, the way he thought.

Sometimes it was as if there was no barrier between them, not even a whisper of difference in who they were. In those moments, Sienna believed that somehow they could have a possible future. She dreamed of fixing the border, solving the problem of the Warlord's bloodlust and the power-hungry Shadow Cartographers, bringing peace to both sides. Surely that was possible?

A ray of light from the moon caught the silver handle of Finn's sword, the intricate patterns reminding her of his allegiances, of how little she really knew him.

She sighed softly and turned to see Jari leaning against the wall, twin swords never far from her hands. A warrior woman, more than Finn's equal here. Jari met Sienna's eyes, her cool gaze an appraisal that found her wanting.

CHAPTER 6

IT WAS STILL DARK when Sienna awakened. Her thick cloak was scant protection against the cold stone but for a moment, she lay motionless, listening to Mila's gentle breath and the deeper sounds of Perry's snoring in the corner of the cave. Jari lay silent a little further away. They had found the cave by starlight after hours of walking and sunk quickly into sleep the night before, muscles aching from the long trek.

The sound of cloth shifting on stony ground came from the entrance. Sienna could just make out Finn's faint silhouette. She slowly unwrapped herself, careful not to wake the others and tiptoed out to join him.

It was cold and foggy, the clouds still dense above them but in the distance, the coral fingers of dawn crept over the horizon, the promise of a new day. Sienna sat down on the outer ledge next to Finn, aware that they had not been alone in too long. There was so much to say, so much she wanted to ask him.

"Morning," he whispered.

Sienna grinned. "Morning." That was as good a start as any.

Finn pointed out into the blackness of the valley below, at the faint shimmer of a river and the outlines of buildings.

"That's the library." His voice was reverential as if he spoke of a temple or another place of worship. "I haven't been here in a long time. Part of me thought perhaps I had dreamed it even existed."

"What's it like?"

Finn reached for her hand in the dark and she took it, holding onto his strength. "It is everything I think the best of Earthside must be. Knowledge, truth …" He turned to look in her eyes. "Beauty."

Sienna could hardly breathe as tension mounted between them. He dipped his head to kiss her—

"Not interrupting anything, am I?" Jari stepped across them, her words mocking as she sat down on the edge, legs swinging out into the canyon below. She had her pack by her side, her two swords strapped and ready to go. She seemed effortlessly poised.

Finn pulled away and dropped Sienna's hand. The imprint of his palm remained and she wrapped her arms around herself, trying to hold onto the moment.

"Not at all." Finn was brusque once more and just like that, the barrier was back between them.

Jari pulled some leftover bread from her pack, tearing off tiny pieces as she gazed out. "It's a hell of a view."

A ray of sun broke through the clouds and lit upon a towering spire of white marble that rose up from a classical courtyard beneath surrounded by a small town of houses and market squares.

Sienna had imagined the ruins of Alexandria laid out before them, evidence of neglect and the burnt-out remains of what had been destroyed by Christians in the fourth century. But of course, life didn't stop when a place ended up here in the Borderlands. Time passed and life would always find a way.

She looked sideways at Finn, his face staunch. In the same way, the sun rose and set every day they were not together, life taking them in different directions.

Finn stretched and stood up. "We should descend the gorge before the sun is high and it gets too hot to walk. I'll wake the others."

He stepped around Sienna, avoiding her eyes and went back into the cave. Mila's groan of annoyance and Perry's low rumble of a voice echoed from within, followed by the sound of laughter.

"He's not for you." Jari's voice was low, as gentle as the sharpest blade that cuts deep to the bone before you even notice. "Finn is a Borderlander, this is his home, we are his people. Remember that."

Before Sienna could reply, Mila came out of the cave entrance, yawning and stretching. "Oh wow, this place is incredible. How did we possibly let this go from Earthside?"

Jari stood up and brushed off her clothes. "You drove it away. You denied its existence. You burned it down and killed its people. You don't deserve it."

She spun on her heel and set off down the steep path, sure-footed on the rocky ground. She didn't look back.

Mila raised an eyebrow. "Okay, then. Someone's grumpy this morning." She looked down at Sienna with a cheeky grin. "You two been fighting over something?"

Sienna blushed as she stood up and flicked the dirt from her clothes.

Perry hefted his pack up onto his shoulders. "Jari's right, though. The grand destruction of the Library of Alexandria is a romantic myth. It declined over several hundred years, the scholars expelled before some of it was burned during the time of Caesar and later under the Christian Pope. But after Alexandria lost its preeminence in the classical world, the library disappeared from history."

Finn laughed. "It disappeared from *your* history, but it began a new chapter right here. Let's go see the Librarian." He set off down the track, Mila following, then Sienna and Perry bringing up the rear.

The path was clear, well-worn by travelers, and the group strung out, giving each other space as they descended into the valley. Sienna looked up as the cry of a falcon rang out, the bird of prey hanging in the updraft as the sun warmed the land. The Library of Alexandria stretched out below, its central buildings like a classical temple winding down to a river with stepped terraces. Around it, the town awakened in the morning light, and Sienna could just make out tiny figures walking through the streets. She wondered about their lives here. How much did they even know of Earthside?

Distracted, she stumbled a little, her feet slipping on loose rocks, her heart pounding as she clutched the stony cliff behind her. Life was fragile on both sides of the border and no magic would save her if she fell off the edge, dashed on the rocks below. She laughed to herself. That would be a really stupid way to die. She stopped looking at the view and placed her feet more carefully as she descended.

The sun was high by the time they regrouped at the bottom of the escarpment by the banks of a sparkling river. Jari lay on a rock, eyes closed, relaxing in the sun. At least she looked relaxed, but Sienna had no doubt that the warrior woman could leap to her feet, swords at the ready, if she sensed a threat.

Finn crouched on the bank and drew in the dirt with a stick, sketching a long rectangle marked with a central box. "The Librarian works in the central hall here." He marked an X in the box. "But we can't just waltz in there, especially with you two." He looked at Perry and Mila. "Fire magic and water magic are forbidden, for obvious reasons with all those books. But more than that, the security is run by a branch of the Shadow Cartographers — the Scryers."

Mila sighed. "They can sense what magic we have."

Finn nodded. "They recruit from here, and when I say recruit—"

"You actually mean force into slavery or worse," Perry cut

in. "I've heard of these Scryers. My father said ..." He shuddered as his words trailed off. He shook his head to clear the memory. "We can just stay out here and wait for you."

Jari sat up. "Don't be a baby. We can get past a few Scryers."

Sienna crouched down next to Finn. "And besides, we have to go together." She pointed at the X in the center. "If the Librarian knows a way to get to the pieces of the map, it's likely that we'll travel from there straight away. I'll need you all with me because I can't come back for you."

Finn nodded. "Exactly." He drew lines around three sides of the main library hall. "The Scryers have outposts here, here, and here and the rumor is that they have some kind of net under the river protecting the water entrance. We can get past them." He looked up at Jari with a dark smile. "We just need a diversion."

Jari jumped down from her rock. "I'm sure I'll think of something by the time we get there."

The group walked along the bank of the river past humble dwellings that soon gave way to grander mansions and then became the bustling hub of the city. The river widened, forded by pedestrian bridges and ferry boats that carried people and animals alike. Street vendors called from market stalls as they passed, hawkers tried to sell them library trinkets. Sienna slowed down to look at some tiny books bound with real leather before Mila pulled her away.

"You can't take anything back, remember. It creates a link back to you, a way for the Shadow Cartographers to find you on Earthside."

Sienna thought of Mila's canal boat, the objects she had on her shelf. "But you—"

Mila rolled her eyes. "I didn't know any better and besides, mine were taken through ages ago." She pointed at the others moving further into the crowd. They funneled toward one of the main gates into the library complex where people moved through a turnstile flanked by guards. "Come on, we have to catch them up."

When they reached Finn and Perry, Jari was nowhere to be seen.

"Where's she gone?" Mila asked, her tone as suspicious as ever of the Borderlander warrior.

"She'll be ready when we need her." Finn pulled them into the shadows of a temple wall within sight of the turnstile. People queued to get through, chatting and relaxed, the gate clicking as each passed. Guards stood on either side looking out into the crowd, paying no obvious attention to what was clearly an everyday occurrence.

Finn leaned down, his voice low. "We need to get through that gate. Each one of us has to pass through the turnstile separately. They keep it moving pretty fast. Watch how the regular folk behave. You can spot the tourists."

Sienna followed his gaze toward a small group of travelers in the long robes of a religious order, eyes wide as they gazed up at the library ahead. One of them hung back, a young man in his twenties. He had a scar down the side of his neck as if something had been carved from his skin. Sienna frowned as she noticed his white knuckles, his clenched fists. He looked as if he was going to run, but then he stopped himself, took a deep breath and stepped toward the gate, waiting his turn at the end of his group.

As the turnstile clicked and the young man stood between the gatehouses, a harsh sound like the caw of a crow burst out. The guards either side moved in a flash, thrusting their spears out, barricading the young man between them.

An audible gasp spread through the crowd and people surged forward to see what was happening.

Sienna moved with them. As she ducked under one man's arm, she caught a glimpse of an impossibly long bony arm with fingers like spider's legs darting out of the gatehouse, wrapping around the young man before dragging him inside.

He screamed, a sound of terror that was cut off almost as soon as it began.

As silence fell again, the guards stepped back, opening their spears once more. One of them nodded at the next person in the queue, a local woman by the looks of the basket of bread on her hip. She stepped forward with confidence, approached the turnstile and moved through. The rhythmic clicking began again as others followed.

Sienna turned back to see that Perry's face had gone white.

"There's a Scryer in that gatehouse," he whispered, eyes wide with fear. "My father told me stories of them when I was young. They take people down into their den, they suck the magic from you, they leave you a broken husk."

Sienna put her hand on his arm. "It's okay, we'll be fine. Jari's going to make a distraction, right?" She looked at Finn.

He nodded. "Absolutely. And we should go now while that Scryer is busy."

Perry backed away. "No, no, not me. You guys go. I'm staying right here."

Mila took Perry's arm. "You can't go back now. If you don't come with us, you'd better learn to love it here. So, man up and get moving. Look like a genuine tourist and they might not even notice how sweaty you are."

Perry clenched his fists, nodded sharply and together, the group stepped into the crowd. Finn waved the others ahead of him as they approached the gate.

"Whatever happens, don't stop, don't turn around. Stay in a line and just keep moving. Wait for us by the statue of the Muses near the main steps."

Mila walked forward, shoulders back, flirtatious smile on her face as she sashayed up to the guards, Sienna behind her, then Perry.

Just as she reached the turnstile, an explosion boomed out across the surrounding rooftops. Smoke billowed out of a nearby house and the crowd surged forward to the gate. Several pushed in front of Mila in their haste to escape the crush. The guards lost their calm composure and stepped back to allow them all through.

Mila went with the flow, surging through with a group of locals.

A little girl burst into tears near Sienna and she grabbed the child's hand, lifting her up into a hug and carrying her through the gate. "It's alright. We'll find your mommy, sweetheart."

Sienna lost sight of Perry in the crowd but she didn't look back, stepping through the gate quickly. As she crossed into a classical forecourt, a woman's voice called out in desperation, "Jasmine, where are you?"

The little girl struggled at the sound of her voice. "Mama."

Sienna spun and handed the little girl over, then turned back to the gate just as Perry stepped between the gatehouses. His face was determined and he looked straight ahead, meeting Sienna's eyes. A smile of relief crossed his face as the turnstile clicked. He was almost through.

Suddenly, the harsh caw of a crow. The metallic slam of spears.

The guards stepped in front and behind, blocking his path.

"No!" Sienna cried out as the bony hand of the Scryer reached out and dragged Perry away.

CHAPTER 7

AS THE HARSH CRY of the crow sounded, Perry tried to summon his magic, reaching for the flame inside. But the bony hand reached out like a pincer and snapped tight shut around him. As it crushed his body and dragged him inside the gatehouse, it snuffed out the flicker of light inside, his scream cut off before it erupted from his throat.

The gatehouse was pitch black inside. Perry couldn't see the Scryer but he could smell its breath, like wet body parts, as rank as a drowned corpse. Its bones creaked as it moved toward him, the sandpaper scrape of its skin on stone. It raked its bony fingers over his body and the violation cut deep into his muscles, into his heart.

He couldn't move. He couldn't breathe.

His father's words came back to him, as they sat by the fire on the Mercator estate so many years ago. *If you ever get caught by the Scryers, you'll wish you'd never been born. Better to die by the fire of your own hand than have them feed on you and suck the marrow from your bones. They don't answer to anyone but the Shadow itself.*

Perhaps it would let him go. Perhaps his magic wasn't strong enough for them to take. Perhaps—

A trapdoor below his feet opened and Perry fell through, his body still immobilized by the curious power of the Scryer.

He landed on straw, soft enough to break his fall but still crackly and sharp. The clang of metal and spikes rose up from the ground beneath, forming a cage around him. The trapdoor snapped shut above, leaving him in darkness.

Perry grabbed the bars, suddenly released from his paralysis. "Help! Let me out of here."

His words echoed back to him. It sounded like he was in a long corridor but he could sense no one else there. It smelled of minerals and water on rock like an abandoned mine and he could hear the faint skitter of a thousand tiny legs. Perry couldn't help imagining what kind of insects collected the pieces of the dead down here. He stood up sharply, pulling himself away from the floor, his skin crawling at the thought of them feeding on him.

Suddenly, a clank of gears resounded. His cage began to move on rails that took him deeper into darkness before light flickered up ahead. Perry gulped as he considered what he would face, whether the light was a blessing or whether darkness would be better.

The cage entered a long hall lit by flaming torches high up in curved brackets. It clanked to a halt next to another, the bars bumping up against its neighbor.

In the dim light, Perry could see a body lying on the straw, head turned toward him. It was the young man who had been taken just a few minutes before.

"Hey, are you alright?"

The man didn't move. As Perry looked closer, he noticed dark patches on the man's skin. They pulsed rhythmically, like a sinister heartbeat and as he watched, one of them moved, crawling slowly, leaving a trail of black blood behind.

This time, there was no stopping Perry's scream as it erupted from his throat.

* * *

Up above, the crowd surged on toward the grand marble facade of the library. Sienna turned to run back to the gate, desperate to get to Perry. A strong hand reached out to hold her back, tight fingers wrapped around her arm.

"Don't draw attention to yourself," Jari's rough voice whispered. "Or you'll be down there with him."

Sienna shook her hand off. "We have to get Perry out of there. You saw how terrified he was."

She remembered the hunt for the Map of Shadows and how Perry hadn't been scared back then, how he had faced skeletal birds and fire-breathing dragons with no fear. How much worse could the Scryers be? She imagined him down there, buried beneath the city. They had to find him.

Finn came through the turnstile and joined them, his expression like thunder. "I saw what happened. There's nothing we can do."

Mila stepped forward and took Sienna's hand. "We're not going on without him. Perry is one of our team and besides, he saved us in the Castle of the Shadow, remember? You can't proceed without Sienna, so I guess we all have to find a way down there."

Finn looked at Jari. "Any ideas?"

The warrior woman rolled her eyes. "Seriously, no one told me this was a babysitting job." She paused. "But there are some tunnels I've heard about. I'll need to go see a contact of mine. Wait by the statue. I'll be back soon."

As Sienna watched her go, Mila led her over to the marble statue of the Muses, nine beautiful sisters joyous in their celebration of music, poetry, song and dance. They sat on its edge watching the sun-dappled square in front of them as locals and pilgrims alike gathered to approach the monumental entrance of the library.

This was a place Sienna had dreamed of, the prototype of the Bodleian in Oxford, a temple to knowledge, a never-ending stream of learning. She should be entering these halls as joyous as the Muses immortalized above them. Yet all she could think about was Perry, broken and empty somewhere beneath.

It seemed impossible that this bright world existed above and yet below lay only terror and darkness.

* * *

Perry stopped screaming. He panted and retched, tears springing to his eyes as he tried to control the panic rising within him. He looked up to the flickering torches above, reaching inside for his fire magic. He would summon it and turn this place into a fiery hell.

But once again, the strange dampening effect crushed the spark, some power that the Scryers used to keep magic at bay down here, a way to control their victims. Perry slumped in defeat.

The sound of rustling and then limping footsteps came from the shadows at the side of the hall.

A spindly figure, nearly as tall as the torch brackets, hobbled out of the gloom. A Scryer wrapped in layers of ragged cloth that covered it from head to toe, dragging in the dust as it moved toward Perry.

He backed away as far as he could into the corner of the cage. "I'm Halbrasse. Please. My father is one with the Shadow. Stop! I'll do anything."

A pressure built in his head as the Scryer moved closer. It didn't need words. It had a presence he couldn't resist, a way to reach into his very soul.

The Scryers had been human once but generations of old magic had wound into their flesh and now they were scraps of skin and bone held together by pure shadow. Annals of the Mapwalkers said that they lived below some of the oldest cities pushed through from Earthside, sustained by the blood that seeped down through the earth and the magic they could drain from those they captured.

As the Scryer reached the bars, Perry couldn't help but fall to his knees as if it pushed him down with overwhelming force. It pulled back its hood and he raised his eyes to look into the face of abomination. Empty eye sockets in a skull covered with rotting flesh. It opened its mouth to reveal a pulsating mass of Shadow leeches oozing over each other in search of food.

The Scryer lifted one bony arm with its long fingers and picked a leech from within its maw. It writhed, tiny rows of teeth searching for something to latch onto. The Scryer stretched through the bars and placed the leech on Perry's neck. He moaned as the foul creature began to bite into his skin, latching on, sucking the life out of him as weakness spread through his body.

The Scryer reached back into its mouth for more of the parasites.

* * *

Sienna couldn't stand it any longer. She paced back and forth in front of the statue of the Muses. "We're wasting time. What if I just draw a map here and now, go down there, get Perry and bring him back?"

Mila sighed. "You know what happens after you use your blood magic. You'll be exhausted and we need you to get us out of here. Plus, what if they capture you as well?"

Finn looked out at the crowds. "She'll be back soon. Jari's good at what she does."

"I bet she is," Sienna whispered.

Even as she spoke, the lithe warrior woman walked swiftly toward them, weaving around people with an unerring sense of her place in the world. Sienna could only wish for such confidence.

Jari pulled a map from her bag, scrawled with chalk marks. She laid it at the feet of the Muses as Finn, Mila and Sienna gathered round.

"There's a gate here near the graveyard that leads into their compound. The Scryers take what they can from corpses in exchange for processing the dead."

"What the hell does that mean?" Mila said sharply.

"You don't have death rituals on Earthside?" Jari spat back. "A lot of people die here. The townspeople of course, and those who travel to see the library. Some religious sects believe that if they die here, they will make it into some Illuminated afterlife. Someone has to deal with the sheer volume of the dead."

"Why not expel the Scryers?" Sienna asked. "Move them somewhere else."

Finn picked up the map, looking at it closely. "They were here first." He looked down at Sienna, his eyes suddenly distant. "And besides, that's an Earthsider attitude. If you don't like something, expel it. As if everything could be so simple."

Sienna flushed at his words, acutely aware of the truth he spoke. But Perry wasn't dead and she wasn't leaving without him.

"So we go in, get Perry and carry on with our mission."

Finn put his hand on the pommel of his sword. He nodded at Jari. "Okay, but we're in charge. Follow our lead." He leaned in close, so she could smell the cinnamon spice of his skin. "No blood magic, I mean it. I don't want to lose you down there."

He pulled away and she nodded.

Jari scowled. "Let's get this over with." She pointed at the main gates of the library beyond, a marble archway covered in flowers, constantly renewed by the pilgrims who placed them as they passed. "The gate of flowers is sanctuary. If in doubt, run for that. The Scryers are forbidden from entering."

They skirted the edge of the library buildings beyond

the grand edifice to the service area. As with any sprawling public complex, it needed an army of people to run it. They lived and died behind the beauty of marble sculptures and hushed enlightenment.

They passed kitchens, the smell of roasting meat wafting from within, reminding Sienna of how long it had been since they'd eaten a meager breakfast on the escarpment above. Steam hissed out of vents and she glimpsed abundant storerooms through half-open doors, terracotta jars full of wine and oil, dried chilis and other spices she didn't recognize.

Behind the kitchens, rows of sleeping huts stretched back, becoming more humble toward the cliff face where the worst of them backed onto the graveyard. At least that's what Sienna supposed it was, but this place was unlike any she'd seen before.

Tiny shrines of different faiths sat around the edges of a raised platform on which three trapdoors sat, two open, one closed.

Jari hopped up on the platform and knelt by one of the open doors. She leaned in and knocked gently against the wooden panel within. "They must take the bodies down this way."

Sienna walked to the nearest shrine upon which trinkets lay in devotion, some carved with the names of those who had passed. In a sense, this practice was no different to the sky burial of Tibetan Buddhism or the Towers of Silence of Zoroastrianism where the body was left out for birds of prey to devour. The difference here was that the Scryers took the living as well as the dead.

She walked back to the platform and climbed up onto it. "Let's go."

Mila tilted her head to one side. "But how do we actually get in there?"

Jari gingerly stepped down onto the other trapdoor. As she put her whole weight on it, the door dropped and she fell into blackness. The door shut behind her.

"Guess that's how," Finn said, stepping forward and dropping through after her.

Mila and Sienna followed suit.

They regrouped in the tunnel beneath the trapdoors. It was colder down here and the air smelled of decay and something else — something that made Sienna's stomach turn. But it wasn't the dead they came for.

Jari and Finn pulled their swords and together, they walked slowly down the tunnel into the heart of the Scryers' domain.

CHAPTER 8

PERRY LAY ON THE straw, his breath weak and ragged as the Scryer placed one final Shadow leech on his outstretched arm. It made a soft caw, then turned to shuffle back into the darkness. He watched it go with heavy eyes, wanting desperately to close them and sink into oblivion but a sliver of hope kept him awake. Sienna and Mila would not leave him down here to die. He just had to hold on a little longer …

The pain was a pulsating wound, his magic draining away with every heartbeat. A death of a thousand cuts as the leeches sucked the fire from him. When the Scryer gulped down the creatures again, it would absorb his magic with their flesh, perfect parasites existing in symbiosis.

There was no reasoning with them, no moral argument that could be made to stop their malevolent consumption. They sought out and devoured magic and somehow, Perry guessed, it made its way back to wherever the source of the Shadow lay. It was strangely comforting to know that a part of him would go back to its origin after he breathed his last. He would give much to see where it lay.

His vision began to narrow, the flicker of the torches dimming as he closed his eyes, a sense of the tide washing over him, cold spreading through his veins.

Then a sound came from the corridor beyond. A scuffle of footsteps.

Too late …

* * *

Flaming torches in brackets lit the hall beyond, giving the cages around the edge a sinister red glow. Finn and Jari entered first in fighting stances, swords held at the ready. Sienna walked in behind them, Mila at her side.

The corridors from the graveyard had been empty, and there had been no challenge to the team's progress so far — no watchers, no soldiers, no protection for those within.

But Sienna did feel a weight pressing upon her, a heaviness that drew her down with every step.

"Do you feel that?" Mila asked quietly. "I just want to lie down and sleep. It's exhausting."

Jari turned. "The Scryers have a dampening effect on magic. They sense it, they drain it. Don't let them touch you." She walked quickly to the first cage. "Perry must be in one of these."

Sienna looked down the line at hundreds of cages, each holding a captive, lying prone on bloody straw beneath. The figure that lay in the closest cage was just a husk of a person, unrecognizable, drained of all life and magic. A sense of hopelessness rose up within her. Were they already too late for Perry?

A clank of machinery sounded in the hall and the cages shunted forward.

"The far end," Finn whispered. "As each drop through, they move along. Perry will be in the more recent cages."

They ran together, footsteps ringing out in the hall. A new cage came through from the tunnel beyond, a little girl this time, her eyes wide with fear, her face streaked with tears. Sienna reached through the bars. "It's okay, we'll get you out of here."

Jari knocked away her hand. "Stop that. We're not here for her, or any of them." She pointed to the hundreds of other cages. "You want to let them all go? Find your friend quickly before we end up like these poor wretches."

Tears sprang to Sienna's eyes as she turned away. Jari was right, of course, they couldn't save every soul.

"He's here," Mila called out from a few cages further up, her voice desperate with concern.

Sienna rushed to her side and Finn joined them. Perry lay unmoving on the straw, dark creatures pulsating on his skin.

"Shadow leeches," Finn said as he tugged at the bars, searching for a way to get inside. "Get them off him. Mila, help me loosen these."

Sienna bent down to kneel next to Perry's head. She reached through the bars, shuddering as she touched one of the fleshy creatures.

"Perry, we're here. Hang on now."

Sienna grasped the leech and pulled. As she tugged, it tore and ripped at Perry's flesh, burrowing deeper. It was part of his body now, no longer just a parasite.

Mila handed her a knife. "Here, try cutting it off."

Sienna edged the blade under the leech, black ooze running from it along with the dark stain of Perry's blood. She pried it off, cutting through its flesh.

A cry of agony rang from the darkened arches beyond the cage, like a wounded bird keening for its mate. A Scryer stumbled from the gloom, its long limbs and ragged clothes brushing the floor. Its skeletal visage of bone and shadow screamed at them, the same black and red blood running over its chin that wept from the leech.

"You're hurting it," Mila said in wonder, then her voice hardened. "Do it again."

Finn stepped forward, his sword held high. "Quickly."

Jari spun away from the cage of the little girl, ready to fight alongside him.

The Scryer rushed them, long limbs flailing as its avian lament echoed through the hall, the screech making the hair on Sienna's arms rise up at the terrible noise. She stabbed at the leeches on Perry's skin, slashing at them, hacking them off.

The Scryer screamed with pain as the leeches shriveled up in bloody clumps, its agony linked to the tiny parasites. Finn swung his sword at it and the blade went right through as if it were just air, trailing wreaths of shadow behind its arc. Finn spun with the weight of the blade and tried again, just as Jari darted in with her weapon. But neither of them could touch the wraith.

It staggered closer to Sienna, long fingers reaching out, its features flickering in pain. Jari ran back to help and together, they scraped the last of the leeches from Perry's skin. They withered on the straw, plump blood-filled bodies shrinking to empty sacs. As the last one dried up, the Scryer gave a final cry and sank to the ground. Finn stabbed at the pile of rags with his sword but it went straight through, ringing on the stone beneath.

As the Scryer disappeared, a click sounded in the hallway and the gates of the cages fell open. Sienna darted forward. She bent to Perry, touched his cheek. "It's okay now. Wake up. It's gone."

His eyelids flickered and slowly, he opened his eyes, his gaze weakened but the Perry they knew was still in there. He opened his mouth to speak—

Just as the loud caw of a crow echoed through the darkened halls joined by another and another until the whole place was a splintering cacophony.

More Scryers coming to defend their home — and their food.

"We need to get out of here." Finn bent to the cage and hauled Perry out, lifting him over his shoulder in a fireman's lift. "Run!"

As Mila headed for the exit, Sienna turned to see Jari lifting the little girl from the cage next to Perry's. The warrior woman scowled and shook her head. "I'm not leaving her. Now run!"

Together they raced back the way they had come, through the tunnels toward the graveyard. But this time, the harsh cawing followed them, the incensed sound of Scryers stumbling, their towering bodies unused to moving so fast.

The team pulled ahead and made it back to the trapdoors in the graveyard. Finn placed Perry gently down on the ground before pulling down the hatch and boosting Mila up into the daylight, followed by Sienna. He lifted Perry and pushed him up into their waiting arms, helping Jari and the little girl next and then finally, pulling himself out of the hole.

They stood panting on the raised platform, the bustle of the library city before them, willfully oblivious to the horrors beneath.

"We made it," Mila panted, bending over to catch her breath—

Just as a long, bony arm reached out from the last trapdoor, catching her hair and tugging her to her knees. From below, the sound of triumphant cawing rose from the darkness.

"To sanctuary!" Jari shouted as she jumped off the platform, the little girl in her arms, tiny face buried in her neck.

Finn used his sword to cut through Mila's hair and Sienna pulled her friend away. Finn picked up Perry again and together they ran back past the kitchens and service areas toward the gate of flowers. Panicked screams rose up behind them along with angry caws as the Scryers pursued their prey.

The group turned into the main plaza, the orderly stream of pilgrims entering through the gate turning to look in the direction of the commotion. Soldiers moved forward with their lances outstretched, faces aghast at the creatures chasing behind.

"Out of the way!" Finn bellowed as they ran for the gate of flowers. Something in the pilgrim mass responded and the crowd parted, allowing them to surge forward. They were so close now.

The Scryer in the gatehouse emerged and the crowd gasped at its soaring monstrosity, the power it exuded as it stalked forward, joining its brethren in pursuit of the escapees.

Sienna stumbled, tripping on the stone steps, falling forward.

She cried out and rolled quickly, just as the long fingers of the Scryer behind reached down for her, raking across her flesh. She looked up into the darkness of its hooded visage and saw something like surprise in its depths, a recognition of her magic. Its caw this time was primal, a deep sound of yearning for her powerful blood.

Mila darted back, grabbed Sienna's hand and pulled her up, onward to the gate, an arch of flowers, a haze of scent and color marking the boundary.

A group of pilgrims stood watching the chase. Some urged the team on, beckoning them to safety. Others were silent, watching with hungry eyes, eager to witness the magical victims dragged back down to the catacombs.

A slender Nubian woman stood in the middle of the flowering arch, her hair white as spun sugar, her face ageless, her eyes deep pools of an unusual sapphire blue that stood out against her black skin. Even as she ran for her life, Sienna sensed the woman saw further than this realm, and weighed greater matters than just their lives in her hands.

The Librarian.

Jari ran through the arch first, falling to her knees, hugging the little girl to her chest. Finn crossed the line next, placing Perry on the ground before turning to reach for Sienna's hand, pulling her over with Mila just as the gatehouse Scryer reached them. It stopped outside the gate of flowers as its brethren gathered behind, tall wraith-like creatures wrapped in rags, long skeletal fingers brushing the ground. They exuded menace, their presence causing a hush to fall over the gathered crowd.

Finn went down on his knees before the Librarian. "Please, give us sanctuary. We need your help for a terror far greater than these can bring. A terror that threatens us all."

The Librarian looked over his head at the ragged Scryers beyond, her blue eyes raking over them with an edge of steel in the depths. It was clear that she hated the devourers of magic and abhorred their power in the outer limits of her realm, but she had little choice.

The gatehouse Scryer took a step forward, right up to the flower gate, only millimeters from the bright fallen petals strewn over the earth. It gave a rough caw like a crow over carrion, a reminder of the balance that must be kept according to the laws of the Shadow.

The Librarian's shoulders slumped and she looked around at the Mapwalker team with a sigh. "I'm sorry, I must ..."

CHAPTER 9

THE LIBRARIAN'S WORDS TRAILED off as her eyes alighted on Sienna and the sapphire blue sparkled as she smiled in recognition. She lifted one regal hand and pointed away from the gate speaking in the rough caw of the Scryer tongue. It was clearly a dismissal.

The Scryers stood for a long second, then turned as one and stalked away, back to the darkness beneath and the hidden inner gatehouse beyond.

The crowd drifted away now the conflict was over, leaving the Mapwalker team kneeling on the ground before the Librarian.

"Thank you," Sienna said. "Why did you change your mind?"

The Librarian smiled. "Your grandfather was my … friend … when he was your age. I would know that titian hair anywhere and I can sense an echo of his power in your blood."

Her eyes grew soft at the mention of the past and Sienna wondered how much more than friends they had really been. She remembered the young woman sketched in her grandfather's journal with such love. Time passed differently out here at the edge of the Uncharted but could this really be the same woman? If it was, she had barely aged a day.

The Librarian waved her arm toward the inner courts. "Welcome to the library. Now, come inside and tell me why you're here. It had better be worth the fury of the Scryers." She looked down at Jari, her arms still wrapped around the little girl. "Leave her with the Sisters of Grace in the fore-court. She will not be sent back down there, I give you my word."

Jari nodded and darted away with the child without a second glance. Finn watched her go and Sienna noticed a smile playing around his lips as he witnessed the warrior woman's long-hidden kindness. It seemed she was not so cold after all.

The Librarian led them inside the classical library, a grand edifice of marble columns with decorative Corinthian scrolls, like a stylized forest of learning. The atmosphere was hushed, reverent, and Sienna glimpsed rooms beyond the columns where scholars studied and pilgrims worshipped at the shrine of the book. Part of her wished she could stay awhile, with nothing to concern herself except the number of pages read each day. But would a quiet life of contemplation really satisfy her now after all she had seen in the Borderlands — and all that was yet to come?

Jari emerged from a side corridor as they passed by. She was alone now, the hand that had clutched that of the little girl now wrapped around the pommel of her sword.

She met Sienna's questioning gaze with a hard look. "Don't even think about saying anything."

They stopped by a pool of crystal water surrounded by ornate fountains with sculptures of ancient Egyptian gods at their center. The high ceiling opened up to the sky above, allowing dappled light to play across the stream. Tropical flowers blossomed, casting their heavy scent into the air and tiny birds flitted between the leaves, their song a sweet note.

The Librarian indicated marble benches under a bower of flowering cherry blossom that provided privacy from the bustling pilgrims. Mila and Finn helped Perry to a long bench and healers came to tend to his wounds. He lay unmoving as they coated his lesions with a salve that smelled of honey and spice.

Servers brought fruit and tea with the fragrance of high mountains and the team sat together with the Librarian as Sienna explained their mission to find the Map of Plagues.

"The Mapwalker annals mention that one of the knights may have crossed over here to the Library of Alexandria. Perhaps he hid a piece in the archives amongst the many manuscripts? Perhaps he sought help from the Librarian of the time?"

The Librarian frowned. "It's possible. We have our own annals, passed down over the centuries, notes about what really happened since history written by men of power portrays only one version of the truth. Those scrolls rest in the oldest part of the library." She took Sienna's hand. "I'll take you to them because of your grandfather."

Sienna smiled. "I know he would have loved to see you once again."

The healers finished patching up Perry, providing a staff for him to lean upon until he recovered full strength. He was pale and drawn, his shoulders slumped, but his eyes had regained a glimmer of their old sparkle.

He shrugged off the help that Finn and Mila tried to provide. "I'm fine, honestly. Just let me walk."

The Librarian led them away from the sanctuary of the pool toward the center of the collection. The architecture changed as they wound their way through corridors of stone, becoming less ornate, more functional. Age had worn down the flagstones they walked upon, leaving imprints of footsteps from the long dead. Ash and the dust of millennia blackened the walls. These inner halls were almost deserted, just a few quiet figures slipping behind columns as they passed.

"There's not much left of Alexandria now," the Librarian said as she led them deeper within, light fading as the windows grew smaller until they were only chinks that let in a sliver of light. "What is left we keep in darkness to protect from the damage of time."

The inner library became a labyrinth of twists and turns until finally, they reached a central room constructed from huge blocks of stone. Shelves hacked from the rock were piled high with hundreds, perhaps thousands, of scrolls. Some were thick, as long as carpets, rolled on the lower shelves, and others light and airy heaped nearer the ceiling. Many looked fragile, like they would crumble to the touch. It was reminiscent of the Illuminated Cartographer's study, but where that was alive and vibrant, lit by reflected sunbeams, this room was cold and barren.

The past could be alive in the Borderlands after it had been pushed out from Earthside, but only if people made it their own. These scrolls were the dead parts of Alexandria, discarded history that the descendants of those Egyptians chose to leave behind. But Sienna also sensed power lying in maps of skin somewhere here, maps made from Blood Mapwalkers like herself.

Jari spun around in the center of the room, shaking her head. "How are we meant to find a tiny piece of a map in here?"

The Librarian gave a knowing smile. "If the map is to be found, I trust it will be." She turned to Sienna. "Your grandfather renewed the pact with the library and I hold you now to the same promise. The dark clouds of war gather overhead and we want no part of it. Leave us be. Take your fragment and then forget you were ever here. Do not mark us on your new maps, do not report us to the Ministry. Let us continue to be forgotten as a piece of a once glorious past so that we can live on for centuries more."

As Sienna looked into the deep blue of the Librarian's

eyes, she caught a glimpse of ancient Egypt, palm trees and pyramids, then the slow death of a civilization that thought it would rule forever. A sense of foreboding washed over her, a realization that everything must die, that every great society must crumble.

"Promise me," the Librarian urged.

Sienna nodded. "I promise."

The Librarian squeezed her hand, then turned to the group. "I'll leave you now. Go with my blessing."

Jari looked confused. "But you can't leave us in here. There's no way we'll make it out of this labyrinth without help."

Finn put his hand on her shoulder. "We're not leaving that way."

Jari flushed, shook her head. "Of course, I didn't … let's just start looking." She walked to a stack of scrolls and began to search.

The Librarian walked to the door and turned one last time as if to fix them all in her memory, then she left, leaving only the scent of flowers in her wake.

Perry sank to the floor with exhaustion and leaned back against one of the pillars. Sienna bent and tucked his jacket around his shoulders. "Just rest until it's time to go."

Mila turned around in the center of the room, hands on her hips, as she examined the racks of scrolls. "There's something here, something more than just vellum and papyrus." She met Sienna's eyes. "Something of skin."

Sienna nodded. "I feel it, too."

She stood and together they walked slowly around the chamber, becoming attuned to the vibrations of the library and each scroll within it. Finn and Jari went to sit next to Perry, watching the women in silence.

Sienna felt a pulse in her blood quicken as they drew closer to one section and Mila stopped next to her with a puzzled expression. They both turned to the shelf and examined the pile of scrolls. They had fused together with time, a tangle of lost knowledge. Mila bent and blew off the dust. It rose into the air, making them sneeze.

"Bless you," Perry said instinctively from across the room before falling into an awkward silence. The phrase stemmed from plague times when the blessing of God was called down on potential sufferers, a ward against disease. Sienna hoped they wouldn't need that protection themselves.

"Let's go carefully and try not to inhale too much ancient dust," Mila joked, breaking the tension. She pulled out each scroll carefully, edging the top ones off the pile and Sienna placed them on the floor. Jari and Finn came to help and together, they emptied the rack, laying out the scrolls in rows.

Sienna noticed that one in particular seemed to emanate with an inner light. It was dirty brown on the outside, as dusty as the rest, nothing special, and yet she felt an urge to touch it. She stepped gingerly around the other scrolls and bent down, brushing her fingertips over the skin.

She gasped as a jolt of energy rushed through her.

She unrolled it carefully on the stone floor. Inside the outer scroll lay a piece of tattered skin, a patchwork of different colors and lines. It was not the skin of an animal and it wasn't like the blood maps that hung in the gallery of the Ministry. This was something hybrid, something knitted from the skin of many and inscribed with powerful blood.

"Is that it?" Jari asked. "Is it a fragment from the Map of Plagues?"

Sienna nodded. "It must be. It's knitted together from pieces of skin, some from plague sufferers and some from a Blood Mapwalker. The knights must have sewn them together, entwining magic with the plague itself to keep it hidden."

As she looked at it, Sienna had the sense of something uncurling deep within the earth, something long buried from ancient times. It fed from the mass graves of genocide and the horrors of war. It devoured the plague-ridden bodies of the diseased and dying.

And now it was awake.

CHAPTER 10

FINN KNELT NEXT TO Sienna and placed a hand on her shoulder. "Are you alright? You've gone pale."

Sienna took a deep breath. "There's more going on here than we know."

He nodded. "But that's always been true and we just have to keep going. So, where next?"

Sienna lifted the ragged piece of the Map of Plagues away from its protective outer scroll. It too had lines inscribed upon it, a simple sketch showing waterways and islands. There was a drop of dried blood on the page, the color of rust partially obscuring the lines of a death's head skull. "The knight had to travel somewhere when he left this place. He must have drawn this and then stepped through it to escape Alexandria. The Librarian kept it with the piece of the map he left behind."

Mila examined it more closely. "It looks like Venice. Does the trail take us back to Earthside?"

Perry pulled himself up from the wall and limped over. "That's not Venice in Italy. That's the Venice of Africa. It's part of Benin on Earthside, on the northern shore of Lake Nokoué."

Finn laughed. "Of course, it's Ganvié Island, the floating city. Like Old Aleppo, it straddles the border, half pushed out from your world into ours. The local Fon tribespeople helped Portuguese slave traders by raiding the villages of other tribes hundreds of years ago. But their religious beliefs prevented them from attacking those who dwelled on water, so the floating city grew out of the homes of those early escapees."

"You know it?" Mila asked.

Finn shook his head. "I've never been but I've heard stories. We'll have to be careful. Its waters cross the border and people are lost between the worlds there all the time."

Sienna folded the piece of the Map of Plagues and placed it inside a waterproof pouch within her jacket. She pulled out the ritual knife that she kept close to her heart, the knife that had spilled the blood of her grandfather. Any blade would do to make the cut, it was her blood that held the power, but the reminder gave her strength. He had never retreated from his duty, and neither would she.

She ran her fingers over the map of Ganvié, calling on the tendrils of her magic as she strengthened herself for what was to come. Every time she spilled her blood and traveled through the maps, a drop of Shadow entered her — a tiny speck, but still, it built up over years and eventually, could turn the Mapwalker to the Shadow side. Some chose never to use their magic after a certain point, trapped on Earthside or in the Borderlands at the point of turning, like Bridget and now her own father. Others chose to give in and become a Shadow Cartographer, embracing their magic in all its glory.

Sienna looked up at Perry. His father had chosen that path, as had Xander, who had been with them on the hunt for the Map of Shadows. She had thought he was a friend but he had betrayed them all.

There were no limits to the use of magic if you gave in to the Shadow and Sienna sometimes dreamed of the possibilities. Back at Oxford, she had always felt so lost and yet over here in the Borderlands, she could be much more than she ever thought possible. She wanted to give in to the rush. A taste of it was never enough, but it was all she could have right now.

Sienna looked up at Finn and Jari. "Make sure you keep hold of my hand." She purposefully met Finn's gaze. "I don't want to lose you."

She bent over the map and cut into her palm with the knife, letting a single drop of blood drip down onto the lines, pooling with the knight's from so long ago. She reached out with the other hand so the team could hold onto her, then she closed her eyes and dived into the map.

In Sienna's mind, the lines became three-dimensional, lifting from the page to form a city stretched out below. This was the moment she craved and Sienna longed to stay right here in the lines between the map and the physical world. If she traveled alone, perhaps she could prolong the time between, but the others were a heavy weight upon her, forcing her back down to the physical world. She could make out boats below on turquoise water, fisherman casting their nets and a tangle of islands that made up the watery city.

The border appeared as a shimmering line and Sienna made sure to come down on the Borderland side. Finn and Jari would disappear if they crossed back into Earthside without traveling through an open portal. No one really knew what happened to those who disappeared but she wasn't about to find out now.

She picked one of the huts on stilts that looked like a place of worship rather than a dwelling and dived down into it.

The wooden hut was hot after the cool inner sanctum of the library. The smell of salt water and drying fish wafted through the air. Sienna heard a slithering sound of scales on wood, then the rapid breath of panic as the team landed beside her.

She opened her eyes, trying to focus even as the nausea

receded. Traveling this way left her weak, especially when she carried this many people. The tiny wound on her palm throbbed and she could almost feel the drop of shadow suffusing her blood as it healed.

She lay inside a wooden hut with a tin roof, the others on the floor around her. The planks on the floor had gaps between them that showed the water beneath. Around the edges of the hut were wooden crates, stacked three high. The slithering sound came from within.

Jari sat up, a half-smile on her face. She looked at Sienna with renewed respect and an edge of fear. "That was crazy. What a way to travel. You must jump around like that all the time."

Mila stood up, recovering quickly. "There's a price she must pay for it."

Jari shrugged. "We all pay, in this lifetime or the next."

As the team recovered, pulling themselves up to sit against the walls of the hut, a hissing came from within the stacked crates.

Finn went to look inside, pressing his face against the slats before pulling back sharply. "That's a lot of snakes."

"Voodoo," Perry said, his voice stronger now. "It's the state religion in Benin and I imagine that's continued over here in the Borderlands. Pythons are revered. There's even a python temple in Ouidah on Earthside. Other kinds of snakes are used in ceremonies."

Finn nodded. "I've heard of these minor sacrifices. They are nothing compared to those performed in the name of Moloch." He glanced over at Jari who had gone still at his words. "But I'd rather not stay in here longer than we need to. Where do we go next?"

Sienna took a deep breath and pulled herself upright using the wall as support. "Let's see if we can pick up the trail of where the knight went next."

* * *

Mila's heart pounded as she put her hand against the door of the hut. She wanted to be out there first, barely able to contain the excitement that had been building since Perry mentioned the Venice of Africa. She had grown up in a London tower-block, a mixed-race foster kid with little knowledge of her birth parents except that her father had been a student from war-torn Sierra Leone. It was further west in Africa than Benin but this was much closer than she had ever been to her possible ancestors.

Waterwalkers, those who could become one with the waterways, were born rarely and many of them disappeared without trace, choosing to remain beneath the waves rather than return to the air. Mila understood that choice. Even now as she looked down between the slats of the hut, she wanted to be in the water below. The channels around the stilts were the real roads and she craved the freedom of traveling at her own speed, darting alongside the sea creatures below.

As she gazed down into the water, Mila suddenly saw movement. Not the shimmer of schooling fish, but something larger, its edges blurred by the ripples of the seabed. Mila frowned. It looked like the outline of a person — could there be Waterwalkers here?

"What are you waiting for?" Sienna's words interrupted her reverie.

Mila shook her head. "I saw something under the— It doesn't matter. Let's go."

She pushed open the door, barely catching a glimpse of the city on the water before a shout of challenge rang out, deep voices blending together as a group of Ganvié tribesmen thrust sharp spears toward her, their scarified faces fixed in a challenge.

Mila reeled back into the hut, knocking into the others as the tribesmen advanced.

"Wait," Finn said, backing away, his hands held out in surrender. "We're on a mission from the Warlord of Aleppo. We have safe passage." He pointed at Jari's facial tattoo of the half-moon. "See, his emissary is with us."

Mila wondered what he was talking about and noted Sienna's look of puzzlement too. That was more than Finn had told them so far and the idea that he might be working with his father was troubling. But there was no time to find out more as the tribesmen quickly bound their hands behind their backs.

The sound of heavy footsteps came from outside on the boardwalk and an obese man waddled into the room. He wiped the sweat from his bald head with a corner of his tunic. It was tied around his waist with a rope from which hung dried pieces of sea creatures interspersed with shark's teeth, pervading the room with a rank smell. The tribesmen deferred to him, shrinking away as if he wielded cruel power over them. Mila supposed he was a priest of some kind.

He squinted at Jari in the semi-darkness of the hut. "You're Aleppo filth. You die first." He looked around at the others. "The rest will be a grand offering to Requin Géant."

Sienna stepped forward. "Please, we don't want trouble. We're here to find traces of a medieval knight, a man in armor who might have come here a long time ago with a piece of a map. It's a danger to us all. Please let us go. We mean no harm."

Mila was sure that a flicker of recognition crossed the man's face at the mention of the knight, and she definitely recognized the name of their god. Requin Géant. French for giant shark.

CHAPTER 11

XANDER SAT SKETCHING ON the edge of the castle wall, looking out at carrion birds as they swooped low over the burial pits. He could look at them now without flinching, ignoring the women who wept below, an unceasing roll-call of death. But the birds … well, the birds were life and Xander could bring life to the beasts he illustrated. If he could only get a skin to draw on. For now, he had to make do with his sketchbook and as his hand moved across the page, he brought the birds to life on the wing, their feathers ruffled by the wind, their beaks open to snatch insects from the air.

He completed one bird and on the opposite page, he began to draw again, using the template of its shape to extend the wings, add talons to its feet and make the beak more like a scythe, the feathers more like blades. Sir Douglas had tasked him with creating weapons from the creatures he could illustrate and with nothing else to occupy his time, Xander filled his sketchbooks with creatures of the imagination.

From his perch this high up, he could see into the walled garden behind the double doors of the children's wing, a quadrangle of green flanked by trees and bushes with colorful flowers to brighten it. A movement caught his eye and Xander watched as a slight young woman with cropped, almost silver hair ran on tiptoes over the grass, her arms raised high as she spun around, her red dress billowing out around her. She turned her face to the sun and smiled. Xander couldn't help smiling with her, the simple joy of a sunny morning. He wished life could always be so simple.

The young woman pulled something from her pocket and bent to the ground, digging a little hole and placing whatever it was within. Xander strained to focus, a frown on his face as he tried to see what she was burying.

She covered the hole with earth, patted it down, then placed her right palm upon it and stretched out her left toward one of the other trees, an apple tree with white blossoms. She closed her eyes and lifted her face again, her mouth set in determination.

A few blossoms fell from the tree as if a gust of wind had caught it.

Then they rained down in a thick cloud, leaving the boughs of the apple tree empty. It began to wither even as the girl lifted her hand from the earth, revealing a tiny sapling underneath that stretched toward the sky, growing at an incredible rate.

The young woman stood, both arms stretched out toward the trees, one growing and reaching for the sky, the other shriveling and fading, its life force drained as the other bloomed. Xander watched wide-eyed at the speed of her creation. He knew that they bred Halbrasse here, raising children with forms of magic unseen on Earthside but this girl was truly incredible.

"They call her Elf." A gruff voice came from the walkway behind him.

Xander looked around to see a soldier, the half-moon tattoo covering a web of burn scars.

"You should see what she can do with insects." The soldier shuddered. "Sir Douglas wants you in the library. Now."

The soldier didn't wait for an answer, just turned and stalked off, his message forgotten already.

Xander sat for a moment, his mind racing. At last, the chance he'd been waiting for. In a place where magic like Elf's was fostered and encouraged, his own talents would surely not be wasted. He couldn't help the grin that dawned on his face as he imagined what he'd find in the library, maybe even the secret books rumored to lie within.

He packed up his sketchbooks into the satchel by his side and jumped down from the wall, jogging into the cold shadows of the castle and winding his way through the corridors toward the library. It lay in the heart of the central tower, protected on all sides by thick walls and magical seals.

Xander stopped at the door to take a breath. This is what he had been promised. This is why he'd given up the Ministry.

He stepped inside and looked up at the soaring shelves around him, stacks of books of all sizes mingled with rolled parchment scrolls and carved stone blocks, metal plates and other forms of ancient knowledge. The border prevented modern technology from crossing over so books were the real treasure. As they were forgotten and discarded on Earthside, they ended up here, abandoned wisdom come to life again.

"Don't just stand there. Come in." Sir Douglas looked up from the armchair he sat in and Xander bit back the gasp that rose in his throat at the man's appearance.

Sir Douglas had been the epitome of English aristocracy, with a military bearing, salt and pepper hair swept back from an angular face, and three-piece tailored tweed suits that made him look as if he'd stepped out of a nineteenth-century painting. The vertical scar that ran down from his right eye to his short beard only served to hint at his rakish past.

But now Sir Douglas looked like a shell of his former self, his skin paper thin and dry as if all the moisture had been sucked from him. His hair and beard were entirely white and the scar looked like it had deepened, sinking into his skull. He still wore tweed but the suit was ill-fitting now, his skeletal limbs barely filling the sleeves. As Sir Douglas waved him in, Xander noticed the dark lines on his hands and wrists, the black marks that crept up his neck — and the tendrils of shadow that seemed to weave around him, obscuring his features before shifting again.

"You've never seen the transition to pure shadow, have you, Xander?"

"I'm … sorry, sir. I didn't mean to stare."

Sir Douglas shook his head. "It's fine, it's not something many witness, but it is your future if you remain here with us, if you help us." He smiled. "To go from the physical body to the realm of pure shadow is the only way to make your power endless."

Xander couldn't speak, he couldn't move. Sir Douglas spoke as if this transformation was something to be desired but all he could see was the bitter and ugly end to a life.

Sir Douglas pushed himself up from the chair. "But you have much to prove and little time. Come with me."

He stalked over to a bookshelf filled with thick tomes with leather bindings and gold etching. The titles were obscure, arcane grimoires and ancient philosophies mingling alongside natural history and principles of engineering. There seemed no order to the chaos of books and Xander found himself leaning closer, trying to work out how they all related to each other.

Sir Douglas pressed against the spines of two volumes and something clicked behind the wall before part of it swung open, revealing a smaller room within.

The hidden library. At last.

"Can I go in?"

"Of course, this is what I promised you." Sir Douglas smiled but his eyes remained dark, the spark within them a black diamond that seemed to suck the life out of the surrounding air.

Xander stepped inside, his feet sinking into a plush carpet embroidered with scenes like a Hieronymus Bosch painting. Demons tortured sinners, their bodies torn on racks while others were burned alive or eaten by hideous misshapen creatures.

There were fewer shelves in here and only one desk in the center. A wooden box sat on one end.

Sir Douglas pointed to the books. "You will find much to occupy you here, many wonders to fill your sketchbook. It is yours to explore. But we have one task for you to accomplish first."

He walked to one of the shelves and pulled down a medieval book inscribed with two interlocking triangles on the leather cover. Sir Douglas opened it carefully revealing a diary of sorts within, handwritten words on fragile ivory paper turning yellow at the edges. He turned the pages until he reached one filled with images.

Rats. So many rats.

But not just any kind of rat. These were giant creatures gnawing on the bodies of the dead. One gazed out of the page, its beady eyes looking out from across the centuries.

Xander shuddered and then bent closer. There were fleas on the page, jumping from the bodies of the rats to gnaw at those who ran from the infestation. There were swollen lumps on the dead and suddenly, he knew what the images portrayed.

Sir Douglas turned the pages slowly, filling Xander's vision with drawings of death and suffering. Of mass annihilation.

"There was once a map that came with this book, but it was hidden, split apart so the island of the plague could never be found. But we will have it soon and these flea-infested rats will be our agents of change on Earthside."

Xander's heart pounded as the scale of possibility sank into his mind. He could only imagine the suffering, the millions who would die if a plague like this was released into the hyper-connected world he had left behind.

Sir Douglas reached over and opened the wooden box, lifting out a pile of skins, each perfectly prepared for the Illustrator's work.

"We need more of the creatures. You will illustrate them on these skins and we will bring them to life in the camps in readiness for the plague." He placed a hand on Xander's shoulder, pushing him down onto the seat. "You wanted to use your magic to create without limits. Well, here's your chance."

It seemed to Xander as if the chill of the shadow sank through his clothes and into his skin. Even as Sir Douglas turned to leave, tendrils of darkness snaked back to hover around the desk. Xander bit his lip and reached for his illustrating instruments with a shaking hand.

Something watched him, something began to insinuate into his brain and it seemed as if the first strokes of the pen were not even his own.

The rats that began to appear on the skins were more grotesque as his mind considered what would make them even more effective. They must run fast and spread wide, carrying the plague faster than ever before. He drew them with snake-like bodies so they could writhe through cracks, carrying their cargo of death into homes. He made them fierce with sharper teeth so predators would not be able to kill them off.

Some part of Xander watched his own hand with horror, a last vestige of his old self despairing at what he'd become. But as the shadow entwined itself around his drawing hand, he couldn't help but revel in his power of creation.

CHAPTER 12

THE PRIEST SHUFFLED BACK to the door, his belt of sea creatures rustling as he walked. "Bring them," he said, leaving without a backward glance.

"Wait, we're—"

One of the tribesmen cuffed Sienna around the head as she blurted out the words. She fell to the floor.

Finn surged forward but two other men held him back. The tribesmen laughed, talking to one another in a language Mila couldn't understand. But she got the gist of it. There was no way these people were letting them go.

The tribesmen pushed the Mapwalker team out onto the boardwalk in front of the hut. Dusk had fallen and the sound of bullfrogs echoed over the lake in the balmy evening. Clouds of insects hovered above the water and fish jumped to catch them from below while swifts darted down to pluck them from the air. Boardwalks stretched into the distance, a labyrinth of walkways between the islands of huts. Some had red or blue tin roofs, others were thatched with straw and mud.

Villagers paddled canoes through the channels, some glanced in their direction, others deliberately avoided a look as they headed home with vegetables and freshly caught fish.

A little boy poked his head out one of the windows,

gazing at the newcomers with curiosity as they passed. Mila smiled at him and he ducked back inside, shy or perhaps afraid of the priest who walked by with such authority toward the rocky shore.

"The topography is strange here," Perry whispered from behind. "Ganvié on Earthside is on a lake but it looks like this place is within a protected bay on the edge of an ocean drop-off. Check out the waves beyond the break-water."

Mila looked past the village huts to the shades of blue fading into the horizon. White-caps dusted the waves out there and her water aspect sensed the resonance of the deep. It called to her and she almost gasped as the need rose inside her.

The priest led the procession all the way across the village to a final walkway that led to a cave entrance where the rising tide lapped against the lip of a platform tethered to the rock. It had shackles embedded within, each pair rusty with age. Crabs scuttled around the edge, some with huge bodies as big as watermelons with long legs that probed the rocks as they passed. These were carrion eaters with sharp pincers that ripped and devoured flesh.

"This is where the children of Requin Géant feed. Perhaps your offering will bring the god himself." The priest clutched the shark's teeth in his belt, crushing his meaty hand against sharp edges until blood dripped down into the water, staining it red. He smiled. "Sharks can smell blood from across the bay, so they will be waiting when the tide floods the cave. But they will need something special to send them into the feeding frenzy that pleases our god the most." He pointed at Jari. "Bring that one."

Two of the tribesmen hauled Jari to the front of the cave where a single pair of shackles lay against a prominent rock. She struggled against them. "The Warlord of Aleppo will have your skin for this."

The priest laughed. "He owes me much for the slaves

we have sent to the Shadow mines and it is Requin Géant that I must appease now. He has not fed of human flesh for too long so you are all a welcome respite before I must offer from my own tribe again."

Finn frowned. "I've heard of this offering, my father does the same at the Tophet, offering children to a god who can never have enough blood. It does no good. It keeps us all in the dark."

The priest shook his head. "The balance must be kept. As Earthside pushes out those who honor human sacrifice, they end up here. We have no choice. If I do not offer, they will take whoever they choose and the village suffers."

Two tribesmen shackled Jari to the rocks at the entrance to the cave, right on the edge of a deeper drop-off while the others shackled the rest of the Mapwalker team to the platform beyond.

The priest took a shark tooth from his belt, chanted a prayer, then slashed Jari's arm. The deep cut began to bleed immediately, scarlet drops pooling in the water around her. The warrior woman already had to crane her neck to keep her face out of the surf. She was panting and gasping for breath in fear and pain and Mila knew it wouldn't be long until she went under. The only question was whether she would drown before the sharks ripped her flesh apart.

Mila could sense the creatures out in the waters of the bay, gathering for their feast. Beyond them, somewhere in the deep, she could sense the giant creature they all worshipped.

They needed to get out of here but Mila had to rein in her power while the team were outnumbered. She could whip the sea into weapons and turn her own body into water, but the others would be injured or worse if she acted too soon. Better to wait until at least some of the tribesmen had gone.

But the priest remained silent alongside his team of men, eager eyes fixed on the water outside the cave, waiting for the sharks they served to come for the feast.

They weren't leaving.

A wave washed over Jari's face and she spluttered and coughed, straining to lift her mouth and nose above water.

"Please," Finn whispered. "Help her."

Mila knew his words were for her. He had seen her wield her water magic before when they had been cornered by the Warlord's men. But they were still outnumbered — she had to wait just a little longer.

A dorsal fin of a shark broke the surface just outside the cave, moving quickly toward the bleeding figure on the rocks.

The priest raised his hands to the heavens. "Take this sacrifice in the name of Requin Géant." His voice echoed around the cave.

"Move, Jari!" Finn shouted.

The shark lunged out of the water just as Jari arched her body backward, pulling her wrist and ankle shackles as far as they would go.

The shark's jaws snapped shut only an inch from her stomach, then it slid back off the rocks into the water circling around to swim back and forth just a few meters away.

The priest clapped his hands in delight. "Next time the water will be higher. We will witness the sacrifice."

Mila couldn't wait any longer. As the waves washed over her feet, she summoned her magic, becoming one with the liquid. Her skin shimmered, expanded and the shackles broke around her ankles.

The priest turned, shock on his face. The tribesmen by his side raised their spears and charged.

Mila reached down to gather handfuls of the sea and spun it into two whips of water in the air. She snapped them at the legs of the men, knocking them off balance so they stumbled and fell into the rising waters.

As they tried to scramble to their feet, Mila spun her whips again, snapping off the shackles that held Perry and

Finn captive. They each turned to the guards nearest them, pushing them under water. The drowning men writhed as they tried to escape but Finn forced one into his shackles, snapped them shut, then turned to help Sienna out of her bonds as Perry wrestled with the other.

Mila turned back to the priest.

He pulled the shark's tooth blade from his belt once more, advancing with eyes blazing. "You dare challenge the priest of Requin Géant? You will pay with the salt of your blood, Waterwalker."

The priest rushed forward, surprisingly fleet-footed for a man so big. He thrust the blade at Mila. As she whipped the air before him, he cut through the water droplets with no hesitation, laughing maniacally as he bore down upon her.

"Help!" Jari's voice was desperate as the shark fin rose in the water before her, the dark grey of its great body visible beneath the waves.

A flash of white teeth.

The priest turned his head in triumph, eager to witness the devouring of his latest sacrifice. Mila charged at him, propelling the fleshy man across the cave so he tripped and fell back over Jari's shackled body, his head dangling right over the water.

Just as the shark rose and bit down with its terrible jaws.

Blood spurted from the priest's decapitated corpse, soaking the warrior woman beneath, pooling in the water by her side. Mila bent down and used the expanding water to snap the shackles from Jari's wrists and ankles.

Jari sprang to her feet, her clothes covered in blood. She kicked at the body of the priest, rolling him into the water. "Go feed your precious sharks, you bastard."

Out in the bay, more shark fins appeared, drawn by the gore. The two tribesmen, now shackled further back in the cave, began to beg.

"Please, we were just doing our duty. Let us go."

Mila turned to see Sienna reaching for the closest one, her friend was ever the forgiving type. But this was no ordinary place, and Mila had the sense that there was more to this hidden city than they knew as yet.

She walked over to stand in front of them, the rising waters now thigh deep. She looked them both in the eyes.

"One chance. Is there an older temple here? A temple for those with my kind of magic?"

One guard looked blank but Mila saw a flash of recognition in the other's eyes. She bent closer to him. "Do you know of it?"

He shook his head. "I've heard of it, but only rumors. The Waterwalkers are said to be extinct but—"

"We're not." The voice came from behind, near the entrance to the cave.

Mila spun around to see a young man pull himself out of the ocean. Water dripped from his body as he stood tall, wearing only a pair of shorts that did nothing to hide his muscular physique. His skin was the color of earth after warm rain and Mila couldn't help but want to run her hands across it. His black hair was cropped short, his eyes wide above angular cheekbones marked with wavy lines tattooed in tiny dots. Mila had read of this scarification, the markings made to honor the water gods.

The young man walked closer, his eyes fixed on Mila. "I'm Ekon, the last Waterwalker left in Ganvié." He reached out a hand and Mila stretched out hers in return. As their palms touched, she felt an electric spark between them, conducted by the water that bound them together.

"I'm Mila. These are my friends — Sienna and Perry, Finn and Jari."

Ekon looked at the group, his eyes resting on the half-moon tattoo on Jari's face. "Do you vouch for them all?" He half turned to indicate the sharks drawing ever closer in the lagoon, a pack of fins breaking the surface as the predators circled. "They still require sacrifice."

Mila took a deep breath, part of her wishing she could just ditch Jari here and now, let her be devoured by the sharks, be rid of her for good. But Finn wouldn't allow that, and they needed Finn.

"I vouch for them all."

Ekon nodded. "You've come a long way and you are of my blood, Mila Waterwalker, so I will show you the temple." He walked to the entrance of the cave, the waves now almost waist-deep. "We must hurry or your friends here will be shark bait." His face hardened as he looked at the tribesmen. "Leave those two. I've seen them watch enough people die down here. This time it's their turn."

He slipped around the pillar at the entrance. Mila hurried after him, Jari and the others right behind as the shouts of the doomed tribesmen faded in the distance.

Holes and crevices pitted the rock wall outside the cave where the water had eaten away at it over time. Giant ferns hung down, casting shadows over the water, the sound of waves against the rock beating time.

There were plenty of places to hold onto as Mila clambered along, trying to keep Ekon in sight as he scrambled sideways along the water's edge. She knew that he climbed instead of waterwalking to enable her friends to follow but she longed to see him slip into the water, his dark skin rippling alongside her own. She had never swum with anyone of her blood before, and now, here he was. Questions filled Mila's mind about whether she could be from this region, whether she once had a home here — and could there still be one?

Ekon turned to make sure she was watching. He gave a cheeky grin and ducked into a narrow entranceway just above the waterline. Mila followed him down a tunnel that soon opened out into a large cavern. Stalagmites climbed toward the roof, glistening with milky white crystals. It was cool and smelled of salt water and the earthy scent of minerals leached from the rocks around.

One wall was carved with wave patterns, similar to the scars on Ekon's cheeks.

"This was once the Temple of the Waterwalkers," he explained. "Our people were abundant, happy. They lived in union with the sea and its creatures." He turned and looked at Mila. "But the Shadow grew strong in our ruler and he traded many of the women for more power. Young men escaped rather than be forced into slavery. Our magic was lost and our people faded into history."

Mila reached for his hand. "Not all of us."

He smiled and Mila felt the moment stretch on, lost in the dark pools of his eyes.

Sienna broke the silence. "We're all facing a threat now, regardless of race or magic or which side of the border we stand on. We need to find the Map of Plagues and we think a knight came here hundreds of years ago. He may have buried something here."

Ekon nodded. "I know of this knight. Follow me."

He led them toward the back of the cave, through a winding passage between dripping walls of rock, emerging into a hollowed-out cavern. A rock in the shape of an anvil sat in the center covered with tiny sculptures made from carved driftwood and dried seaweed. Some were desiccated, shriveled with age and others were juicy and wet, recent offerings from one who still honored the ancestors.

Mila stepped up to the altar, feeling an urge to kneel here and pray to those whose blood ran in her veins. She reached for one of the sculptures and brushed the seaweed gently. This place felt so familiar.

Ekon pointed to the rocky wall behind the altar. "Is that your knight?"

It showed a mural of a man in unusual armor and a helmet painted in the natural colors of kelp and coral, faded by time. Next to him, a Waterwalker stood with a crown on his dark curls, his black skin shiny with new paint, the colors renewed over time in a sign of respect. The men stood shoulder to shoulder against a backdrop of a city that was nothing like Ganvié, a pyramid in pride of place marked with the black lines of a death's head skull.

Sienna walked closer to the wall. "He certainly looks like a medieval knight, and that image on the pyramid was also in the library. Perhaps he hid another piece here with the help of a Waterwalker?"

Mila examined the city behind the men. "It looks almost Egyptian, but how can that be?"

Ekon circled the altar to stand by her side. "As land is pushed over from Earthside, forming new places in the Borderlands, the same happens underwater but not at the same rate. This city is beneath us, an ancient place of mystery buried by the ocean perhaps thousands of years ago. Our ancestors worshipped at its altar but it is unreachable by any except our kind." He pointed at the Waterwalker king. "If he had to keep something safe, it would be in the city below."

Mila turned to face him, her eyes bright. "Will you take me?"

CHAPTER 13

MILA AND EKON SAT on the edge of a pool at the back of the cave. It had clearly been formed by ancient tools, each inch of hard-won stone carved by those who spent their lives in the dark, the sound of metal on stone ringing in their ears.

"Have you been down there before?" Mila asked.

"Many times." Ekon ran his hand over the stone and into the water, his flesh shimmering, turning to liquid as he touched it. There was evident pleasure on his face, a sense of longing for the deep that Mila recognized. On Earthside, she fought the urge to swim, to call on her water magic and sink into the canal or the river or the ocean, because each time she used it, she exchanged a piece of herself with the shadow. But now, she could give in to her desire, sink into the blue, become one with the waves with no guilt. The penalty was still the same, but somehow, it didn't matter any longer.

Something changed along with her body when she became water. Sometimes she wondered whether she might turn into a sea creature if she remained underneath long enough. Her magic made her part of the water, and she didn't know how long she could stay down for. She had never tried it for too long, aware of the seconds ticking away and the drops of shadow turning in her blood.

Mila glanced sideways at Ekon. He didn't seem bothered by fear of what might happen. He seemed entirely at ease with his magic. His dark skin was several shades deeper black than her own, his body sculpted with well-used muscles. She couldn't take her eyes off him.

Ekon met her gaze. "My ancestors came from Africa on Earthside, you know." He shrugged. "At least that's what they told me when I was growing up in the camp. Perhaps we're related."

Mila turned her face away to hide her blush. *I hope not.*

Sienna came to kneel next to Mila at the edge of the pool. "Are you sure you want to do this? We don't know what's down there."

"But I do." Ekon's voice was confident, sure of himself. "I've been down to the ruined city many times." He looked at Mila, his glance hesitant. "We should be fine. I mean there are creatures down there, things that came over from Earthside. They should be as extinct as this city but they still survive here. Don't worry, I'll keep an eye out for them."

Sienna put her hand on Mila's arm. "You don't have to go."

Mila looked down into the deep blue pool. All she wanted was to swim away, to lose herself in the depths — and some time alone with Ekon would be good, too. But Sienna didn't need to know that. She sighed. "We need this piece of the map."

Sienna nodded. "But we don't know for sure that it's down there."

Finn stepped forward, his deep voice resonating in the chamber. "The mark on the pyramid matches the Librarian's map piece. All the signs point to it being down there and we have no way of exploring the city without you two. It must have remained untouched for so long because there are so few of your kind."

Your kind. Finn's words echoed in the chamber and Mila caught a tightening in Ekon's jaw at the implication.

They were the 'others' here. She and Ekon were outsiders and in a small way, it thrilled her. Mila had always felt like the odd one out and usually, in the Borderlands, she was lumped in with the rest of the Mapwalker team. But suddenly, she had kin. There was another of her kind here. Was this her true home?

Mila swung her legs around and put her feet into the water. The shimmer of blue washed up her legs as they became fluid, edges blurring into the pool. She caught Ekon's eye as he looked at her, his eyes darkening as he followed her curves into the water. Men had looked at her body with desire before, but never like this. Ekon saw her true self.

She looked up at Sienna and Finn. "We'll just go and have a look, then report back. We won't be long."

Ekon pushed himself off the edge of the stone rim into the pool, sinking quickly, his body quicksilver flashing beneath. Mila pushed herself off to join him, leaving her friends behind.

The water was clear turquoise and as they descended, the outline of the sunken city became clearer. It was nearly ten kilometers long and half as wide, bisected by a grand causeway lined with statues and a colonnade that led to the looming pyramid in the center.

Ekon darted in front of Mila, his features obscured by the water as if a layer of silk had been laid across his flesh. She had never seen herself in a mirror underwater after the change but she imagined that she must look the same way. Smooth lines gliding through the water like a water sprite. She wanted to touch him, to see what his body felt like down here.

"Isn't it incredible that this was built nearly ten thousand years ago?"

Mila froze, hanging in the water, stunned that she could hear Ekon's voice.

He frowned. "You can hear me, right?"

Mila nodded. "I didn't … I didn't know you could speak underwater. There's never been anyone for me to talk to before."

Ekon laughed, the sound muted, pressed down by the weight of the water above them. "It seems there are a lot of things you didn't know about *our kind*."

He said the last words in an approximation of Finn's voice and Mila giggled.

A giant manta ray suddenly flew out of the blue toward them, black wings gliding on the current, gaping mouth open to filter feed. Ekon flipped over on his back, letting the wash move over him as it passed, then gliding in its wake. Mila loved to see him enjoy his watery body. She had spent so much time in denial of her true nature, it was refreshing to see someone so at home in his. There was a sinuous beauty in the way he moved and she wondered if she could ever be as graceful.

Ekon gave a cheeky grin as he turned in the water, catching her eye. He swept his arm over the drowned city before them.

"Some say it was buried under water when the ice caps melted, thousands of years before known civilization. After the memory of this city faded on Earthside, when it was written out of your history, it ended up here."

"But we've been told that the border was only drawn a few hundred years ago."

Ekon raised an eyebrow, a ripple in the water as he shook his head. "It may be your Mapwalkers strengthened what already existed, but there are things in the Borderlands that you haven't seen on Earthside for many generations. There are many levels to history — and to truth."

They swam down to the grand entrance gate, flanked by statues of ferocious warrior gods, swords held high in multiple hands reminiscent of the Hindu god, Kali.

As Mila swam closer to examine the weapons, a huge

shadow passed overhead, blocking out all light, turning the water to inky black.

Ekon grabbed Mila's hand and pulled her quickly behind the pillars of the colonnade. She peered out, wondering what could make such a shadow in the water.

A massive shark cruised by above them, at least four times as big as a Great White. Its colossal tail caused a current as it swept back and forth through the water and Mila had to hold onto the pillar to stop herself being washed away.

They had been in its way only seconds before. Mila's heart pounded as she considered the near miss. She had mostly waterwalked in the canals and inland rivers of modern England, threatened only by discarded metal or entanglement in fishing lines, as well as dealing with the occasional Feral Borderlander who crossed over. But she had never even considered the hierarchy of the deep.

Perhaps she didn't belong down here after all.

As the massive shark faded into the deeper blue, Ekon swam out from behind the pillar into the main causeway again and hovered above the huge cobblestones. "I'm not sure if the shark could even sense the signals we give off down here. I don't know anyone who's ever studied us, do you?"

Mila thought of the Castle of the Shadow and how they probably tested people like her and Ekon. Perhaps there might be children there with water magic, too. She pushed down a shudder at the thought of what studying them might mean.

She shook her head. "No, but let's not start now. We need to get out of here before dark."

They swam on past ornate columns, each decorated with a statue of a giant beast, some recognizable on Earthside, some strange hybrids she had only seen in mythological books. Mila floated beneath the statue of a lion, its paw resting on a globe, its mane eroded by time. Tiny fish swam in and out of its mouth, open in a roar, darting between its teeth with no fear. It looked as if it could step down from its pedestal and prowl this ancient city again.

They passed over mosaics, intricate tiles of brilliant color revealing scenes of city life — market stalls filled with produce, and busy street vendors with skin colors from all over the world. A huge octopus dominated one tableau, its tentacles reaching out, spiraling to the edge of the design. As they swam on, the mosaic displayed a scene from what must have been a brothel, naked bodies entwined with lust in all kinds of positions. Mila swam a little faster, trying to control her rising blush which of course, Ekon wouldn't even see down here.

He looked over at her, his smile cheeky once more. "I think you have this kind of thing on Earthside, right?"

"Umm, of course. But not usually displayed as a mosaic on the high street."

Ekon laughed. "Some say the city was destroyed because of sin. The people loved pleasure too much and they paid for it eventually."

"Like Sodom and Gomorrah?"

Ekon shrugged. "I've never heard of that. Remember, our histories differ even though we share common ancestry."

They swam on until the central pyramid loomed high above them. It was more imposing as they approached and light filtered down from above cast an eerie gloom over the place. It exuded dark energy, as if it pulsed with something inside. Mila had seen pictures of the Egyptian pyramids and those in South America, but somehow this was different. A wave of apprehension swept over her and she edged closer to Ekon. He had been down here many times and he had returned safely. She would be fine as long as they were together.

Toward the bottom of the pyramid, the density of the city increased, as if people crowded closer to the object of their worship. Temples crammed up against tiny dwellings and shops that must have once teemed with people.

In front of the pyramid there was an open area with huge stones in the shape of a circle, a magical symbol in so many cultures. Mila thought of The Circus back in Bath, a long way from here, for sure, but perhaps this pyramid had once been a powerful gate.

Two giant stele flanked the final approach to the pyramid, stone slabs covered in strange writing, somewhere between cuneiform and Egyptian hieroglyphics, a hybrid language lost along with the city.

Mila ducked down to look at it more closely and traced the lines with watery fingertips, wishing she could read the script. What would it tell of the history of this place? Would it warn of future destruction? She hoped the Mapwalker archaeologists could come down here and find out more at some point.

Ekon pointed toward the peak high above them. "There's a ceremonial entrance at the top of the pyramid, but that was blocked up a long time ago. I found another round the back. There are rocks barring the way, but I think we could get in there together."

A shiver ran down Mila's spine. Strange, because she was never aware of the temperature of the water once she swam within it, her flesh altering to become part of the liquid, but his words made it suddenly cold.

She followed Ekon around the side of the pyramid — straight into an army of statues. Some carried spears, others knives, others curved throwing implements. Some stepped forward with menace, others stood to attention waiting for command. They were of varying sizes, some little more than children, others taller than the tallest man on Earthside. They gazed up the slopes of the pyramid with empty eyes.

The statues were green with algae in places and fish darted in to eat from their flesh, picking pieces from their skin. A sea star crawled across the face of one soldier, questing tentacles poking into the nasal cavity as it traveled across the dead stone.

A group of statues stood in their own battalion with wings folded on their backs like dark angels ready to take flight. Mila called back to Ekon. "Are there winged people in the Borderlands?"

Ekon shook his head. "I've never seen them, but that doesn't mean there aren't any. I haven't traveled much, to be honest. Not like you."

"We don't have them on Earthside, at least not anymore. Only in stories and myth." Mila looked closely at the angels, searing them into her memory. These were real once, perhaps they still were.

No matter how many times she came into the Borderlands, there was always a surprise to look forward to. On Earthside, everything had been mapped. There was little of the wild left and technology meant that you could find anything on the Internet. It was a miracle, enabling people to see into worlds they would never visit on their own, but it also meant there was no mystery left.

The things down here had been lost to Earthside before technology could capture them, before cameras, before anything more than oral storytelling. These creatures had been passed down in the tales of myth, but to see even statues of them was a thrill.

Mila swam between the ranks of statues, looking up into their faces. They were all individually sculpted, each with a slightly different expression. The level of craftsmanship was incredible, further evidence of this advanced civilization.

She turned in the water to look up at the pyramid from the perspective of the soldiers. The dark lines of the stylized death's head stood out in different colored stone and at its center, a pile of rocks where the entrance must be.

Ekon followed her gaze and nodded. "That's where we need to go next. Are you ready?"

Mila looked up at the symbol of death, the entrance at its center. What choice did she have? They couldn't go back without investigating further. She nodded and together, they swam toward the entrance.

CHAPTER 14

MILA KICKED AND SWAM ahead of Ekon, trying to ignore the looming symbol that surrounded the entrance. The boulders had clearly been placed there to stop people entering and over the years, the rocks had fused together with coral and layers of silt. Together, Mila and Ekon generated small whirlpools of water to lift the detritus of years away and once the rocks were revealed, they began to shift those too. Mila was fascinated to see how differently Ekon lifted. She used her watery hands just as she would her solid flesh on the surface, whereas he floated a tiny wave underneath the rock and then brushed it to one side with a sweep of his hand.

He caught her watching him and shrugged. "I guess neither of us was taught the proper way to use our skills."

"I like your way better." Mila copied Ekon's actions and together they moved the rocks with little effort.

Mila swam through the narrow entranceway first, suddenly aware of the tonnes of rock above her, wondering if this was such a good idea after all. The sound of the ocean faded away as she went deeper within, the clicks of fish feeding on the coral, the call of whale song all muted now. It was as if the atmosphere of the ancient culture still remained, sucking all sound within as panic rose inside her.

Just as she was about to turn and swim out again, the small entranceway opened out into a chamber big enough to park a huge truck. It was dark with only a glimmer of light seeping in through the tiny entrance.

The chamber tapered away into blackness and Mila stopped in the water column, all her senses telling her to flee. It was too dark, as if the dead pyramid sucked all living things into it.

She felt a cool touch on her arm, like the fingers of a corpse. She yelped in fear.

"It's only me," Ekon said. "You're jumpy as hell."

"It's too dark." Mila's tone was annoyed, but mainly with herself. "We'll never find anything in here."

Ekon opened his hand and a green glow rose up from his palm, a whirling mini tornado of sparkling emerald and silver.

Mila couldn't help but smile. "Bioluminescence. How did you do that?"

Ekon shrugged. "I've always been able to do this. Try it yourself."

Mila opened her palm, conjuring the water with its microorganisms, drawing it to her. She could spin rain into whips, so why shouldn't she be able to spin water down here into a bioluminescent torch?

She concentrated on whirling it above her palm, drawing in particles until it began to pull light from Ekon's own.

"Hey! Enough already."

They laughed together and for a moment it felt less cold, less like a tomb.

They swam deeper into the pyramid, holding their bioluminescent lights up high. The chamber narrowed and then narrowed more until it was a slender tube heading into the depths of the pyramid. Mila swam slowly, remembering that Egyptian pyramids were full of traps and dead ends to confuse robbers, and tombs the world over had curses guarding what lay inside.

They finally reached the grand inner chamber, green light reflecting off statues of many-handed gods in each corner.

A stone sarcophagus sat in the center. Mila darted to it, brushing layers of silt from the surface. A six-pointed star was carved into the top, more like an occult hexagram than a Jewish Star of David. Curious. Mila frowned.

"This looks similar to the one in London, but how could that be? This city is thousands of years older."

Ekon moved around the other side, examining the edges of the lid. "Time moves differently here, you know that. As Earthside pushes things out, our world shifts."

Mila nodded. "And Mapwalkers can walk through gates that link to different times. Perhaps one of the plague knights ended up here."

"I guess he couldn't get back home."

"Or perhaps he found a reason to stay." Mila couldn't help the blush that rose up her cheeks.

Ekon broke the moment and used a whirlwind of water to widen a crack. "Help me open it."

"What if it's dry inside and we flood it after so long?"

Ekon shook his head. "I think whatever is in here is long gone."

Together they inserted watery fingers underneath the edges of the lid and lifted it with a waft of their hands, floating it down beside the sarcophagus.

A soup of deep reddish-brown rose from its stony interior. Mila couldn't smell underwater but she darted away, not wanting to touch the fetid remains of whoever had lain here so long.

Ekon created a series of little whirlwinds in the water to corral the foul substance into one corner, keeping the particles separate but leaving the heavier, more dense material inside.

They both peered into the sarcophagus. On the bottom lay pieces of what may once have been bone, some jewelry, brooches … and a lead box marked with the same stylized death's head skull.

Mila looked at Ekon. "This has to be it."

As she lifted the box from inside, the sound of rushing waters came from above.

Ekon looked up, confusion on his face. Then realization dawned.

He grabbed Mila's hand. "We have to go — now."

As they swam for the exit, stone blocks moved above them releasing a huge dump of sand from the roof. It just missed them but it swirled up in the water, making it impossible to see.

Mila clutched the box in her watery hand as Ekon urged her on, confident in his sense of direction. But as they reached the final chamber, a massive rock fell from the ceiling and pinned Mila's leg to the ground.

She screamed in pain, pushing at the immense rock with futile hands as agony blazed through her. She pushed the box at Ekon. "You need to go before we're both trapped here. Take this."

Ekon knelt next to her and brushed a hand over her forehead, soothing her. "Think water," he whispered. "You *are* water. You cannot be pinned down. No rock can trap you."

His words cut through her pain, shifting perspective as she understood. Mila closed her eyes and visualized her body like Ekon's, liquid in motion. The weight shifted from her leg and she opened her eyes to see that she had slithered out from beneath it. The pain was gone.

She couldn't believe it. It was amazing what she had learned from Ekon in such a short time. Part of her was angry that no one had shown her this before, and a part of her wondered how much more she had to learn.

They swam out of the pyramid into the open water above the city as rocks tumbled down in front of the entrance, covering it once more, blocking the way into the tomb within.

Mila took a deep breath and shook her head. "That was close. How did you learn about your skills?"

Ekon smiled but there was an edge of regret in his eyes. "I was pinned once, just like that, but with no one to help me, no one to tell me what I should do. I lay alone for three days, and it was only in the depths of delirium that my perspective shifted. Perhaps one of our ancestors whispered it across the veil. It worked and now you know, too."

"I wonder what else we can do."

They smiled at each other, suddenly aware of their potential.

Mila looked back across the city and up to where they needed to go next. Back to the surface, back to her friends, back to responsibility.

They began to swim back up, keeping an eye out for sharks, and as they lifted away from the city gates Ekon reached for Mila's hand, their watery fingers entwined as they swam back to the entrance.

* * *

Sienna paced back and forth next to the pool of water, looking down into the darkness every few seconds, wishing for Mila's return.

"She's going to be okay." Perry sat by the edge of the cave, leaning back against the stone, his lanky frame relaxed as they waited. "Mila wouldn't follow him into danger. She knows better than that."

Sienna stopped and knelt by the pool. "But she's never met anyone like Ekon. She doesn't know how far she would go for him." She couldn't help but glance over at Finn. They still hadn't been able to find time alone to talk about whether there was anything between them, anything more than an unrequited mission romance. Jari kept close to him, and she was certainly more than just a fellow traveler.

Finn smiled. "Ekon will look after her. She's special and he knows that."

Jari snorted. "We can do without them both. We just have to—"

"Look!" Sienna shouted with excitement, as twin shadows appeared in the dark blue waters below, growing larger as they rose to the surface.

Mila's head broke first and a moment later, Ekon surfaced beside her. They beamed at each other, hands still entwined until they realized the others were crowded round the pool. They broke apart and quickly clambered out, their shimmering outlines solidifying once more into smooth skin.

"Did you find anything down there?" Sienna asked.

Mila held out a metal box. "This was within the pyramid in a stone sarcophagus that looked just like the one in London."

Sienna lifted the box and placed it down on one of the rocks. "How do we open it?"

Perry walked over. "Let me have a look." He cupped his hands around the metal, summoning a subtle flame, an exploratory spark. He closed his eyes for a moment, then frowned. "I just need to soften the metal a little without burning whatever is inside."

A moment later, he took his hands away, smiling with triumph. Two of the rivets had loosened in their sockets, the metal sides collapsing in on themselves revealing a piece of map within.

Sienna prised it loose and unfolded it with gentle fingers, sensing the same vibrations as the other piece from the library. She pulled it from her inner pocket and fitted the two pieces together. The ripped edges matched and she imagined the long-dead knight pulling it apart, hoping that he was doing the right thing.

What was the right thing now? Find the other pieces of the map or destroy these two here and now? Burn them to cinders and brush the ashes into the water to sink into the deep. No one could find the plague island then, no one could find a way to send the disease back to Earthside.

But something held Sienna back. Something about the way Finn looked at the pieces she held, as if his life depended on them. She had to find out what was going on and the only way was forward. Find the next fragment, the final piece of the map, and then face whatever came next.

There was no way the Shadow Cartographers would stop now. The final piece lay ahead and that is where the real battle would begin. She hoped Finn would be by her side.

The others gathered close to look at the pieces.

"Where next?" Jari asked, her no-nonsense tone breaking the silence. "Where's the final piece?"

Perry checked the inside of the metal box. "There's nothing in here, no indication of where it might be hidden." He looked at Sienna. "So where do we go?"

Mila cut in. "I saw something down there on the sarcophagus that might help. A six-pointed star, but not a Star of David. It was more like a hexagram, an occult symbol." She dipped her finger in the water and drew a star with droplets of liquid. "I've seen it before in a translation of the Emerald Tablet, popular in medieval times as a Hermetic text. It means 'as above, so below.'"

Finn frowned. "But how does that help us know where to go next?"

"Perhaps it's the other way: as below, so above." Mila drew the symbol again, reversing the triangles.

Jari stepped closer, biting her lip as she examined the marks. "There is a city of air, built into the hanging rocks of a lost canyon, a place so far out in the Uncharted that few dare to travel there."

Sienna could see the apprehension on her face. They didn't have any other clues for the next location, but what could possibly scare the warrior woman so much?

CHAPTER 15

As Finn sketched a map on the ground of how they might travel to the city of air, Ekon reached for Mila's hand and led her to the corner of the cave.

"You could stay." His voice was soft, tentative. "You've only just arrived and I know we've just met, but … I want more time and I know you do, too. Imagine what we could discover about our magic together."

His words echoed deep inside Mila, calling to a part of her that longed for home. Perhaps home was not a place, after all, but a person. Someone who understood her dual self, someone who saw beyond her magic to the woman beneath.

Part of her longed to say yes, to give in to this heady feeling, but if she stayed, if she used her magic the way Ekon did, she would soon be lost in shadow. They would be together, but they would also change into who knew what. The Waterwalkers had all but disappeared, living beneath the waves perhaps, or lost down there in the deep. Was it worth the risk for such a short time together?

* * *

"Mila, what do you think of this?" Sienna called over, frowning as she saw how close her friend stood to Ekon, how she could barely tear her eyes from the young man.

She looked at Finn that way sometimes, although he could barely look at her at the moment. He was hiding something, but she still didn't know what.

Mila turned, her fingers still entwined with Ekon's. "What is it?"

Sienna pointed down at Finn's rough map showing Ganvié surrounded by water and then the trader city, the approximate location of the library and a mountain further east. "Does this look like any of the maps you've seen back at the Ministry?"

Mila walked over and bent closer. "The distances are more spaced out on our version but it looks about right. Is it enough for you to travel through?"

Sienna gazed at the rough lines, letting her magic probe at the edges of it as she imagined the map as three-dimensional, a world she could walk upon, a land she could travel across — or fly over.

Mapwalking was still a mystery, but with every journey she learned more. She had sketched a map like this in the abandoned asylum of Poveglia and traveled through it, but she had been alone, and it was only a short journey. This was some heavy lifting and the more magic she used, the more the shadow entwined within her — and she was beginning to hear it call her name. The sound was a long way off but when she traveled it became louder, as if the shadow flew beside her. The drops of darkness in her blood expanded like the headiness of alcohol, as if she was intoxicated by it and all she needed to do was let it wash over her and she would be free.

"Sienna?" Mila's voice broke into her thoughts.

"Yes." Sienna nodded. "It's enough. I can take us through, I'm sure of it."

Finn and Jari gathered up the packs while Perry carefully wrapped the box to take with them. Sienna slipped the pieces of the map inside her jacket and pulled out her ritual knife. She cut into the still-healing wound on her palm, letting her blood drip onto the stones and mingle with the salt water. She placed her hand on the sketched map, becoming one with the contours of the earth.

She reached out her other hand for the others.

Finn, Perry and Jari gathered around, laying their palms on top but Mila stood apart. She stepped closer to Ekon and wrapped her arms around him. He pulled her into an embrace and for a moment, they clung to each other.

Then Mila stepped away. "I'm sorry. I have to go, but I'll come back. I promise."

Ekon nodded, disappointment in his eyes. "Travel safe, Mila Waterwalker." He turned and dived back into the pool, disappearing into the deep blue, leaving only ripples in his wake.

Mila took a step toward the pool as if she would follow him down there, her fists clenched. She sighed and turned back to the team, reaching out a hand to place it on top of theirs.

Before she could change her mind, Sienna closed her eyes and leaned into the map, pulling the others with her. A second later, she was flying above the floating city of Ganvié, the silhouettes of sharks circling below. As she rose higher, she could see the shimmering border and then the plains of the Borderlands stretching away before her, mountains in the distance.

She focused on the city of air that Finn had drawn for her on the ground and described for them all. A place built high above a tropical forest, with soaring pinnacles of rock. Her focus changed and the passage of time and space below shifted.

Suddenly, the air chilled around her.

Sienna shivered as dark clouds gathered, obscuring the land below. Wind buffeted from all sides and she lost her sense of direction. Panic rose within and her breath came fast. If she traveled accidentally over the border, Finn and Jari would be lost into the mists between the worlds, a place that no one returned from.

She spun around, desperately trying to see through the gathered fog, but all she could see were shadows twisting through the grey, black streaks that drew closer every second.

Then the voice called her name, the one she feared above all else because she longed for it.

Sienna.

The mist swirled clear in one direction, opening a path to the Castle of the Shadow below. Its twisted turrets spiraled high into the sky and at the top of one, a ruby light glowed like a welcoming hearth or a drop of blood.

She could dive down there right now.

Sienna wanted to and if she had been on her own, perhaps she would have gone. But the weight of the others pressed down upon her and Sienna knew she had to take them as far from here as she could. The Castle of the Shadow offered only death for them, or perhaps something worse.

She turned away and the mist closed around her again, cutting off the route down, leaving behind a sense of desolation, that she had missed a chance for something just beyond her reach. The voice grew softer as Sienna dived down through the mist, unsure as to whether she was falling or flying until suddenly the world around her was all shades of green and the shadows withdrew.

Pillars of limestone rose up toward the sky, rope bridges swung between them and on the edge of one pillar, hanging out over the forest, Sienna saw the ruins of a temple that Finn had suggested as their landing point. She dived down toward it and as her feet touched rock, she let the others go and collapsed to the ground, sinking into the welcoming darkness.

* * *

As the world stopped spinning, Perry opened his eyes. He couldn't focus at first, vertigo and nausea making him dizzy, his stomach clenching in protest at the rough trip. Something had happened as they traveled. Following Sienna through a map was usually like stepping through a waterfall, briefly violent and then another place, but that journey — Perry took a deep breath — that journey was like standing under the drowning water and being hammered into rock.

Shades of vibrant green shimmered and slowly came into focus as he sat up. The others lay around him on a stone platform, some kind of ritual circle on the edge of a cliff. Towering pinnacles of rock rose around them with trees growing on different levels, thick foliage obscuring what looked like cave dwellings. Mist gathered in the spaces between the pinnacles, obscuring how far up they must be. A strange cry echoed through the mist, the call of a predator hunting.

A groan then retching sounds behind him. Perry turned to see Finn on his hands and knees coughing and Jari beside him, both almost green with nausea but otherwise okay. Mila leaned against a huge stone statue of an eagle taking flight, rubbing her forehead as she tried to breathe deeply, the fastest way to get through the travel sickness.

Where was Sienna?

Perry stood on shaky legs, turning slowly, heart pounding as he remembered a voice in the mist calling for her. Could she have possibly—

Then he saw her, lying prone behind what looked like an altar on the very edge of the cliff. He stumbled over and knelt by her side.

"Sienna!" He shook her shoulder, turned her over and couldn't help the gasp that escaped his lips. Beneath the skin of her neck and up onto her face, tendrils of black wound through her veins, evidence of the shadow. But Perry had never seen it this bad, except on those who lay in the wards of the Ministry, lost in a shadow coma until they passed beyond the edges of the world.

He pulled up her right sleeve, then the left. Darkness coiled through her skin, whorls of blood corrupted with shadow. He had to tell Mila. They had to get her back to the Ministry.

He began to rise but Sienna gripped his arm, her eyes now wide open.

"Don't," she whispered. "Wait a moment."

As Perry watched, the black marks faded away and moments later, only her pale skin remained.

"How did you do that?"

Sienna shook her head. "I don't really know—" Her eyes widened in fear. "Down!"

She pulled Perry toward her as huge talons swooshed over his head, the cry of a giant eagle echoing around the pinnacle as it swooped back up to the sky above. A sky that was suddenly filled with a convocation of giant birds.

They dived, one after another, talons as large and sharp as scythes.

Perry and Sienna pulled themselves flat against the altar, using the stone to shield themselves against the plunging birds. Perry peered around the edge to check on the others.

Mila huddled behind the statue, but Finn and Jari were out in the open, still on the ground. Finn rolled to his front as one dived for him. The creature couldn't pierce his protective leather coat and flew away.

As another dived for Jari, she rose, twin swords in her hands, shouting at the sky. "Come get me, you bastards!"

An eagle dived for her, talons aimed at her eyes.

She slashed at it, swords tangling in its feathers as she went down under the weight of the creature. It pecked and slashed at her and she screamed as a warrior in battle as they rolled across the flagstones toward the edge of the cliff.

CHAPTER 16

Finn grabbed Jari's boot, pulling her back, even as she fought the creature on top of her.

Another eagle dived for Finn, its cry that of a predator who knows it has won. As the talons struck him, he was driven away from Jari, fighting his own battle even as she struggled under the weight of the eagle as it dragged her toward the rim of the sacred area where mist obscured the drop below.

"Enough." Perry stood up and raised his hands.

The black tendrils in Sienna's flesh reminded him of the cost of their magic, but Finn — and even Jari — were part of the team now and they had only mortal weapons to defend themselves. He didn't have to like them, but he did have to save them.

He summoned fire from within, the burning sensation rising inside until it burst out of his palms into white hot balls of flame.

Perry ran toward the warrior woman, catching her outstretched hand and pulling her away from the edge even as he threw the fireball into the side of the eagle. It caught fire, its feathers burning as it shrieked in pain, freeing its talons from Jari's clothes. It tumbled off the edge of the cliff, a three-meter-wide fiery death.

He spun around and hurled another fireball at the eagle attacking Finn, the blow driving the creature off its prey momentarily. Finn rolled away and ran quickly back to Jari, huddling over her as Perry stood protecting them both, hands raised to the sky, palms burning with almost blue flame.

The gigantic eagles circled above, wary now. Perry watched them, turning as he noted the passage of the largest. It dived once more, then another came from the opposite direction.

Perry waited, his muscles taut as he held himself in check, waiting, waiting …

When he could feel the wind of their descent on his face, he spun around, whipping his flames into a burning pillar then thrusting his arms out wide, creating a towering vortex of fire. The second eagle burned up almost immediately, plunging down to dash onto the stone beneath.

For a moment the largest eagle appeared more like a phoenix, its whole body alive with flame, its beak open to tear apart its prey. Then it too dropped to the flagstones, feathers burned and body roasted, the smell of scorched flesh in the air.

As the flames died down and the smoke from their bodies swept over the side to join the mists below, Perry stood once more, arms raised to the sky, challenging the flying eagles above. Those that were left, circled and then flew away, their cries echoing across the pinnacled valley until it was quiet again.

Perry dropped his arms and sat down heavily on the flagstones, a wave of exhaustion flooding him as the magic dissipated, leaving an emptiness that almost brought tears to his eyes. His shoulders slumped, his mind whirled. He would have fought on until he had been consumed by the flames. Part of him wished the eagles would come back, just so he could feel that surge of power again. In that moment, he understood why Xander had chosen the shadow side.

"Come on, Jari." Finn's voice was desperate.

Perry turned to see him wiping blood from the warrior woman's face, but her wounds were deep, gouges from the talons across her chest, through her armor, along her arms. Her eyelids fluttered and she tried to get up, hand reaching for her sword.

"Rest now. It's okay. They're gone." Finn calmed her and Jari lay back, her breathing a harsh rattle.

"We need medical help." Mila walked over from behind the statue. As she reached them, she squeezed Perry's hand, gratitude in her eyes.

Sienna stumbled over from the altar and sat down next to Perry. They were weakened, but they were still together.

The sound of a slow clap echoed across the sacred ground.

Perry tried to stand but his legs were too frail. The others could barely move either. They were helpless.

The slow clap grew louder and an old man stepped out onto the sacred ground, his face grim and set in craggy features. He wore a feathered cloak that dragged along the stones as he walked toward them. Behind him, a group of soldiers emerged from the trees, each one wearing a helmet in the shape of an eagle's head with a cruel beak spiking from the front.

The man stopped clapping. "No one has killed three of our sacred birds at one time for a generation. No one has ever killed the alpha male." He pointed at the still smoldering body of the biggest bird. "These are Haast's eagles, extinct many centuries ago on Earthside. There are a few left here." He looked pointedly at Perry. "Even fewer now."

Mila stood and faced the man. "They attacked us. We only defended ourselves."

The man pointed at Perry. "No, he defended you all."

Perry noted a strange look in the man's eyes, the look of someone starving who had finally found a good meal.

The man smiled, the stony expression on his face

dissolving into friendship. He held his arms out wide. "Welcome to Aetofolia, the eagle's nest. I am Aguila, ruler of this eyrie. You have passed the test of entry even before you were challenged, so come inside. Rest." Aguila nodded toward Jari. "We have medical help for your friend." He gestured for the soldiers to come forward.

Perry felt Finn tense beside him, a coiled spring ready to explode into action, but there was nowhere for them to go. In one direction there was only sky and mist. In the other, soldiers and perhaps help. Perry noticed the way Aguila looked over at his hands, scanned his body for evidence of magic, and he knew a reckoning must come. He glanced over at Sienna who had shrunk behind Mila. As long as they didn't realize what magic she had, they might be alright. At least for a while.

As Finn relaxed behind him, opening his hands in a sign of surrender, Perry nodded. "Thank you. We gladly accept your help."

* * *

Sienna watched Perry walk forward and clasp Aguila's hand, assuming leadership of the team with the natural confidence she had seen before in his father. But then she noticed the slight delay in his step, a halting stride that spoke of the weakness that came after using magic.

They were all fragile right now.

Jari and Finn were both wounded by the giant birds, Mila was exhausted after Ganvié, and her own mapwalking sucked the energy from her. Sienna knew she faced a challenge ahead, too. Somehow she had managed to dampen down the shadow inside, but Perry had seen the black lines on her skin. He would have to tell Bridget and her father, and she needed him to, because she couldn't do it herself. It might mean the end of her mapwalking before it had even really begun and she wouldn't give up the heady experience easily. But something was different with her. Somehow the shadow leached inside her at a faster rate than the others. Sienna remembered the voice in the mist that wanted to keep her inside the map.

Perhaps that had been its goal all along.

She pulled her sleeves further down over her hands, praying that the black lines would not re-emerge.

Mila took her arm. "You okay?" she whispered, as they walked behind Perry and Aguila toward the rock face carved with a giant eagle. The soldiers jogged behind, one carrying Jari and two others flanking Finn with careful respect, instinctively noting his ability to fight even when injured.

Sienna nodded. "Just a little fatigued after traveling." But as she took another step, she felt the world spin, her stomach clench with something like vertigo and her vision begin to narrow.

As Perry and Aguila stepped up to the rock face, the carving of the eagle split open revealing stone steps leading down into darkness. Sienna thought she saw the mist of the shadow curling out from the depths, undulating toward her with the head of a serpent. Panic rose inside, her breath coming faster and faster as she tried to control the dread rising inside.

They could not go down there.

The world turned to mist and Sienna fell to her knees as the serpent reached her, jaws gaping, fangs bared, swallowing her into the dark.

* * *

Sienna sat bolt upright, heart pounding as she imagined the jaws of the snake closing around her throat. But she found herself sitting up in a soft bed, luxuriant covers around her, a lamp casting a golden glow around the room.

"It's okay. You're safe."

His voice was soft, gentle and Sienna turned to see Finn sitting in a padded chair by her side. He wore a new shirt, no longer ripped and stained with blood. He had a dressing across his right collarbone, just visible as it wound up his neck. Sienna was suddenly aware of how close he was, how his lips were only inches from her own, how she just wanted to be in his arms. But there was so much unsaid between them now.

He reached for her hand and squeezed gently. "How are you feeling?"

"What happened?"

"You fainted just as we entered the eyrie." Finn got up and poured some water from a jug into a glass and handed it to her. Sienna drank deeply, suddenly parched, as he continued.

"You gave us quite a scare, but I know it takes it out of you to—"

Sienna put a finger on her lips and he stopped. They didn't know who was listening down here and if anyone found out about her own blood magic, they might as well give up their quest right now.

"I know it takes it out of you to — travel." Finn sat down again in the chair. "Perry has told of how *he* mapwalked us here, after Aguila enquired as to how we arrived on the sacred platform."

Sienna raised an eyebrow. "Perry's magic is truly all-encompassing."

"Indeed. Mila's sleeping next door and Jari is in their medical wing. They have special balm for eagle talon injuries, so she's going to be alright."

"And Perry?"

Finn sighed and leaned forward, chin resting in his

hands. "We haven't seen him since they led us in here nearly twenty-four hours ago."

"I slept that long?" Sienna shook her head. "We need to get moving. The last piece of the map must be here somewhere. We'll find Perry on the way out but we have to complete that map before the Shadow Cartographers find it."

Finn frowned. "Sienna, there's something I need to—"

A creak from the corner and the large door opened.

Mila walked in, her stride strong again. "About time you were up. Guess what I found out?" She sat on the end of the bed, eyes bright with the thrill of discovery. "The eyrie perches on the top of one of the pinnacles but there's a staircase down to the forest floor below."

"That must be hundreds of meters down?"

"Further than that." Mila grinned. "There's a tomb at the base, a tomb they say the ancestor lives in, a tomb marked with a special symbol." She drew the two interlocking triangles on the covers.

"As above, so below." Sienna smiled. "So we just need to get to that tomb. The final piece of the map must be there. Then we can go home." Her voice trailed off as she caught Finn's gaze, his eyes serious. Going home meant they would be apart again. But there was more distance between them this time than mere geography.

Jari.

Sienna still didn't know what the warrior woman was to Finn but she certainly complicated what had once seemed simple.

"You'll go as soon as you have that third piece?" Finn's voice was halting, his question more of a statement. "You'll just take them all back to Earthside?"

Mila nodded. "That's the plan. There's no way the Shadow Cartographers can find the island with only one quarter of the map, while we might be able to stitch together some options, find the island and destroy it or at least remove all traces of the way to get there."

The door creaked again. Jari stood there, her arm in a sling, her head bandaged, her face still bruised and puffy. She looked every inch the warrior and Sienna was suddenly aware of her own slim frame, sitting in a soft bed with nothing more than tenuous magic. No wonder Finn didn't look at her the way he used to.

"We'll help you finish your mission." Jari stared straight at Finn as she spoke, her eyes a silent challenge. As Finn hung his head, Sienna wondered once more what he was hiding.

Suddenly the deep base sound of drums beat through the air, the vibrations shaking the lamp beside the bed.

Finn looked up, his eyes wide with concern. "It's a call to worship, a call to sacrifice."

Mila and Sienna looked at each other as realization dawned. There was only one of their team missing, the one person who would be considered a powerful sacrifice to the gods.

Perry.

CHAPTER 17

As the drums beat a rhythmic pulse, Mila paced the room. "We don't have much time. We need to split up." She looked at the others in their weakened state. "We're going to have to fight to get to Perry so Finn and I will go up to the sacred area. Sienna, you and Jari go down to the tomb, find that piece of the map and we'll meet you down there with Perry."

"I can fight," Jari said, her jaw clenched with barely restrained anger.

Finn stood up and walked over to her. He grabbed her wounded arm, pressed into the bandage. She exhaled sharply, the pain making her almost double over.

"No, you can't. But you can protect Sienna." Finn adjusted his sword. "I trust you two will manage to get along?"

Sienna hesitated. She didn't want to be alone with the warrior woman. If she was honest, she was scared of her. The half-moon tattoo on her face was a permanent reminder of the side she worked for, and the fragile peace that held their little team together would be over as soon as they had that final map fragment.

Jari nodded. "Of course, we're not children." She took a breath. "And Perry saved my life, so you need to get him out of there." She looked over at Sienna. "You good with that?"

Sienna nodded.

The drums began to speed up, the beat now double time.

"Let's go." Mila grabbed the jug of water as she headed out the door, closely followed by Finn. He glanced back one more time and Sienna met his gaze, seeing concern in his eyes. He turned away and the sound of their footsteps heading upstairs was lost in the beating of the drum.

Sienna pulled off the bedcovers and dressed quickly while Jari gathered their packs. Then together, they headed into the corridor and down the staircase into the dark.

* * *

It was busy on the stone staircase that wound back up to the sacred ground as people from all over the eyrie hurried to witness the sacrifice. Mila kept her head down as she ran up the stairs with Finn close behind, no one paying them any heed. They blended in here, the color of their skin making them part of the mix of races that made a home in the heights of the pinnacle.

People streamed in from corridors that led out from the central staircase and Mila wondered how deep into the rock this city of the air penetrated. As they ascended, she noticed carvings on the walls, intricate designs of eagles soaring over treetops, plunging gorges and waterfalls beneath the towers of stone. Then pictures of sacrifice, figures of men and women, even children, pegged out on the sacred ground while eagles pecked at their soft bellies, dragging out their entrails while the crowd cheered around them. Nausea washed over her and Mila redoubled her pace.

At the top of the staircase, a wide doorway stood open with a vista out over the flagstones to the horizon beyond. The giant eagles once more circled overhead, their cries filling the air even as the gathered crowd clapped along with the drums, faces eager for spectacle.

Mila and Finn pushed their way through to the front of the pack, standing on the edge of the stone circle as a phalanx of soldiers marched Perry forward, chains around his ankles, his hands wrapped in some kind of fireproof material.

They had taken his only weapon.

Aguila, priest of the eagles, stepped out onto a ledge above the crowd and held his hands up to the sky. The drums stopped.

"This man killed three of our sacred birds with the gift of Prometheus. Now, he must pay the same price."

Mila gasped at the reference. Prometheus had stolen fire from the gods and as a punishment, he had been chained to a rock where an eagle pecked out and devoured his liver every day, and every night, it was renewed so he could suffer once again. Now Perry would face the same fate.

* * *

The staircase grew colder as Sienna and Jari descended, the flagstones less worn and older looking as the torchlight faded. Clearly, few people came down here, preferring to live their days up in the towering city of the eagles. There were only a few lamps and the steps between them were shrouded with shadow. The drums faded after a while and soon, the only sounds were their footsteps and their breathing.

Jari had led the way at first, but Sienna noted that her breath came faster now, her breaks longer on the ledges where they rested on the way down. Clearly, she was in great pain, but she wouldn't admit it.

Sienna counted the stairs for the first three hundred or so but then she'd lost count, unable to concentrate as the pain in her leg muscles burned and she clenched her teeth with every stride. Clearly the Mapwalkers needed step classes in preparation for missions, and the thought of Perry trying such a thing made her smile. She pushed aside the pain and concentrated on their task. Find the map fragment and be ready to travel when the others arrived at the tomb.

If they made it back.

After what seemed like an age, the light began to change in the dark of the staircase. A natural green permeated the golden glow of the lamps and as they descended further, it lightened more until they reached a ceremonial archway that opened up to the forest floor.

Jari leaned against a pillar carved with vines, berries and birds. "Just … a minute." Her face was pallid, her skin slick with sweat.

Sienna pulled a flask of water from her bag and offered it to her. Jari took it and drank deep, then handed it back. Sienna took a sip herself and looked around the grove before them. Clearly the people of the eyrie didn't fear whatever lay below, only what flew above. The grove was well-tended with patches of wildflowers dancing in the breeze. The sun lanced through the tall trees around them, dappling on the grass.

A path of stones studded with precious gems of many colors wound into the forest. Metal torch holders stood either side shaped like the heads of eagles. It was clearly a ceremonial way.

Leaving Jari resting behind her, Sienna followed the path into the shadow of the trees. Birds sang in the boughs overhead and the forest smelled of pine and sandalwood with a faint hint of apples. It should have been tranquil and peaceful but Sienna had a sense of foreboding, perhaps worry for the others, perhaps an overriding concern about what the Map of Plagues could bring down on them all.

She turned a corner to find an ancient chapel nestled amongst the trees. It was simple, built of the same stone as the pinnacle itself and as sunlight danced across its timber roof, Sienna caught a glimpse of flowers and limbs of trees entwined into the structure itself. It must have been here a long time, maintained by the people of the eyrie.

As she walked closer, Sienna noticed that the wide oak door was marked with the symbol of two interlocking triangles. She heard a scuff of boots on stone behind her and turned quickly, expecting to see Jari walk around the corner. But the forest fell silent again.

A cloud passed overhead and the chapel was cast into shadow. The stones, which only moments before had seemed welcoming, were now the cold blocks of a prison. Limbs from the trees above loomed like a threat as Sienna walked to the old door and pushed it open with a creak.

It took a moment for her eyes to adjust to the gloom. The old timbers let only a glimmer of light inside but as the room became clearer, Sienna could make out a sarcophagus carved from the same stone as the pinnacle and the chapel itself. It had some similarities to the one she had seen on the video footage of the London plague pit, but this one was carved with swooping eagles and the entwined branches of the forest. There was a stark beauty to the place, giving her a sense of perspective, as if only the bigger things mattered. Not the minutiae of daily life, but the questions that impacted humankind — on both sides of the border.

Sienna stepped closer to the sarcophagus, well aware of how far the knights had traveled to split the map apart. If the third piece was truly here, she would be responsible for bringing it almost back together again.

Could she really trust those in the Ministry with the fragments?

If the plague island really did hold what they thought it did, a weapon of such power could be used by either side to wreak havoc on their enemy. The Borderlanders were people, just as much as those on Earthside. But those on this side of the border still remembered their homes, and that drive could be more powerful than anything else.

She put a hand on the stone lid of the sarcophagus, trying to sense whether she should open it or just run from this place and forget it ever existed.

A creak made her jump and turn in haste.

Jari stood in the doorway, her twin swords silhouetted against the sun, blocking the path out again. "I'll help you with that." Her voice was a dark promise and Sienna couldn't help but shiver as the cold of the chapel pierced her heart.

* * *

"Chain him." Aguila pointed to the sacrificial altar and the guards dragged Perry to it, lifting him kicking and shouting onto the stone, securing the shackles to each corner. The cry of an eagle pierced the air, a hunter spying its prey.

Mila assessed the scene quickly, counting the guards, checking for where other soldiers might be. Behind them, the crowd continuing to surge from the staircase, more and more people blocking the route back down. She clenched her fists, her right hand holding tight to the jug of water.

"This is hopeless," Finn whispered, his face crestfallen.

They were completely outnumbered. There was no way to fight their way out of here and escape down the staircase, especially with Perry so weak and unable to use his magic.

No way out behind them and before them, only sky.

Mila looked out at the blue horizon and remembered one of the carvings on the wall of the staircase. A river, winding through the valley below the mist. It was a long way down — perhaps it wasn't even there at all — but it looked like their only chance.

"Do you trust me?" she whispered back.

Finn nodded. "Of course. I've seen you fight before."

"Then trust me to hold the guards off while you free Perry, and jump when I say jump."

Confusion flashed across Finn's face as Mila gave a wicked grin, her heart pounding with excitement as she ran full tilt into the center of the sacred area straight toward the guards.

They turned with swords raised, ready to fight.

As Mila ran, she summoned her magic from within. She threw the jug of water into the air. It rained down droplets of water which she spun toward the guards like a hail of bullets.

Two fell to the ground, wounds already bleeding. The others were driven back, leaving Perry exposed on the altar.

"Stop them!" Aguila's voice rose high above the cacophony of the crowd, who shouted with excitement at the expectation of a bloody fight beyond the usual sacrifice.

Mila pulled the drops of water back into a whip, spinning and whirling, driving back the other soldiers as Finn rushed to cut Perry from the altar and drag him behind the stone.

As soon as she saw they were free, Mila stepped carefully back toward the edge of the cliff. She found herself laughing as she spun the whips of water out and around the advancing soldiers. This was possibly her craziest idea ever and Sienna wasn't even here to witness it.

"Drive them from the edge and the eagles will have their fill!" Aguila raised his arms to the sky, calling to the giant birds. "Dive, my lords, and claim your sacrifice."

The soldiers pushed forward, swords outstretched. Mila whirled her whips just enough to keep them from moving too fast, while she stretched out her left hand over the edge of the cliff.

"What are you doing?" Finn shouted. "Are you crazy?"

Mila ignored him, sensing the water below. There was a river down there, a powerful rushing body of liquid and it called to her, reflecting back the magic she held inside. Like called to like and her power could be far more than she ever thought it could be. Ekon's face came to mind and what he had taught her in such a short time. He would laugh with her at this, he would join hands and dance in the water too.

For now, she would have to do it alone.

Mila summoned the water from the river below, calling up a towering pillar of spinning blue and white froth. It didn't quite reach the edge of the platform. She spun the whips faster, then risked a glance down. It would have to be enough.

"Jump!" she shouted at Perry and Finn.

Finn frowned and shook his head. "No way."

Perry stumbled away from him to the edge of the cliff, knocking little stones out into the abyss. "I've had enough of this place."

He leaned forward and threw himself out into the blue as two of the great eagles dive-bombed after him.

CHAPTER 18

A S T H E E A G L E S ’ C R Y echoed around them, Mila channeled her magic into the pillar of water, hoping it would be enough. Moments later, she sensed Perry's weight land upon it, but the water level dropped immediately lower and she could feel her magic start to weaken.

Mila spun her whips one final time, then used the water to provide a cushion as she jumped off the edge. "Now, Finn!"

She saw Finn's look of panic just before she fell beneath the level of the platform, then his tumbling figure above her as he jumped after, his cry a curse she hadn't heard for a long time.

They landed either side of Perry who lay cradled in the white water, his eyes fixed on the eagles that circled just above them, wary of their strange passage.

"I've had enough of being captured and tortured for my magic," he said. "Once we get that final piece, we're going home and I'm retiring to become some kind of archivist."

Mila snorted. "Yeah, right. Just as you've finally worked out how to use your fire to such effect?" She nudged Perry in the ribs. "You're tired, that's all."

"Can you get us out of here, please?" Finn's voice was clipped and Mila could see his skin was pale. Then she remembered how much he hated water as memories of the sea serpent under the volcanic city on their last mission flooded back.

Mila tuned into the flow of the water, using her magic to lower them gently toward the river below. The cliff beside them was hung with ferns, and wild purple orchids poked out from the greenery. She picked one as they passed by, its colors a reminder of beauty in the moments before they had to get moving again.

Further down, a graveyard of coffins hung from the rock face supported by woven liana. Each was painted with symbols of the sky and birds and Mila wondered what happened when the wood rotted away. Would the bodies fall to the river beneath or did the eagles come and take their share? Sky burial was part of Buddhist and Zoroastrian tradition on Earthside, so it made sense for it to be practiced here in the eyrie.

When they reached the bottom of the cliff, Mila used the water to deposit them carefully on the bank before returning the liquid to the rushing river. She dipped her hand back in, watching as her skin turned translucent. She sensed that this tributary flowed to the sea and some part of her wanted to dive in and just go with the current. Perhaps she would find her way back to Ekon again.

"I can't see the main gate, or anything that looks like the tomb of an ancestor."

Finn's words broke through Mila's reverie and she pulled her hand from the water, remembering Sienna and the map. She shook her head to clear the thoughts, exhaustion creeping up on her as the adrenalin of magic dissipated.

"We can walk around the base of the pinnacle. We're bound to hit it at some point." Mila looked over at Perry. He stared glassy eyed at the rock face, his body slumped. She frowned. He looked like a broken man. The Borderlands could do that, but she needed him to find his strength again, or they would be in trouble.

* * *

As Jari walked inside the chapel, Sienna turned back to the sarcophagus and touched its rough surface. It was pitted with age, discolored by years of the faithful running their hands over it, perhaps seeking a blessing, perhaps calling down a curse. Which would she find here?

"Help me lift the lid off." Jari positioned herself next to Sienna and together they heaved, thrusting the heavy stone away. It opened a few inches before they had to drop it.

"Let's wait for the others," Sienna said with a sigh, rolling her shoulders, trying to loosen the tight muscles. She could still feel residual tiredness from her mapwalking.

"No," Jari snapped back. "Try again."

Jari seemed on edge so Sienna tried again and this time, they managed to open it a few more inches. The gap was wide enough for an arm to fit through. Jari didn't wait, she stuck her hand down into the darkness and felt around. The sound of scraping nails over stone, the rustle of some kind of material as Jari grimaced with disgust at what she raked through.

Then she smiled with satisfaction and pulled out a small lead box with a hinged lid.

Sienna held out her hand. "Let me look at it."

Jari held it close to her chest, eyes flashing a warning as she clutched the box tightly.

Sienna shrugged. "We can wait until Finn comes if you like. But I need to verify the piece of the map against the others at some point before we leave this place."

"You have the other two pieces here?"

Sienna nodded. "Of course." She pulled the waterproof packet from her inner pocket, fingers brushing against the hilt of the ritual knife. While it was reassuring to have a weapon of sorts, she knew she was no match for the warrior woman, trained and experienced in warfare of all kinds. She could only hope that the fragile bond of their ramshackle team held just a little longer and that Finn, Mila and Perry made it here soon.

"Lay them out on the lid." Jari pointed to the top of the sarcophagus.

Sienna opened the packet and gently eased the two other fragments out, unfolding them and smoothing them down onto the stone.

Jari jiggled the lid of the box, tugging the two edges apart until they began to separate. She pulled it completely open to reveal a folded piece of patchwork skin inside.

"It looks like a match," Sienna said, barely able to contain her excitement.

Jari tipped the box so the piece of the map lay with the others. Sienna carefully opened it out, eyes widening as she saw the detail upon the skin. An island infested with giant rats feasting on its human prey as bulbous sores erupted from their skin.

Jari reached out and edged the piece closer to the others. It was clearly part of the whole and the map was only missing one final fragment now, which lay in the hands of the Shadow Cartographers.

"We've done it." Sienna smiled. "Now we can just wait for the others and get out of here."

"Is that them now?" Jari looked toward the door, head cocked as if she had heard something.

Sienna looked in the same direction, confused at first and then aware in that last millisecond that Jari reached for her sword.

The warrior woman swung the pommel of the weapon at the back of Sienna's head. A dark pain exploded.

As she sank into blackness, Sienna heard Jari whisper, "You're just as much of a prize as those plague pieces, Mapwalker."

* * *

Mila jogged into the clearing. Dark clouds scudded overhead and the entwined limbs of the trees above made it a realm of shadow with the ancient chapel at its center. An oak door lay open a few inches.

"Sienna!" Mila called out as she ran to the door, aware that Finn and Perry were only a few steps behind.

She pushed it open but even as she entered, Mila knew that it was empty. The atmosphere was charged, like the aftermath of a thunderstorm, but there was only dust and old bones here now.

A dark scowl marred Finn's handsome features as he walked carefully around the stone sarcophagus, noting patterns in the dust on the floor. Drag marks. A few specks of blood. His expression changed to something like recognition.

"What is it?" Mila tried to push down the fear rising inside. "Where are they?"

"I'm so sorry." Finn shook his head. "I thought she would wait for me, that I'd be able to—"

"To what?" Perry grabbed Finn's arm, knuckles white with tension. "You knew she was going to take the map pieces?"

Finn shook him off, strode to the other side of the room and turned to face both of them. "I offered to trade the map pieces for my niece, born in the Castle of the Shadow. You remember that hellhole?"

Mila took a deep breath. Of course, how could any of them forget that place of blood and suffering?

Finn continued. "I promised to get the map pieces but I also made my help conditional on you all being safe, crossing back over to Earthside with no harm."

Mila kicked at the door, slamming it into the stone with a shudder. "Now that bitch has all the map pieces *and* Sienna, a powerful Mapwalker whose blood they'll harvest and use to reshape the border. Nice one, Romeo."

Finn sank to the ground and knelt in the dirt, his face a mask of despair. "I know where Jari is taking her."

* * *

The sound of rushing water dragged Sienna out of a nightmare of screaming eagles with bloody talons. Her head thumped with pain. She opened her eyes to see the river running clear beside the hull of a little wooden boat. In the center, Jari paddled with her good arm, first one side, then the other, keeping the vessel in the middle of the stream. The air smelled sweet and pink cherry blossom rained down in a gentle breeze. It should have been idyllic.

Then Sienna remembered.

She lunged for the warrior woman, rage driving her forward. But ropes pulled her up tight and Sienna slumped back into the curve of the hull.

Jari turned her head, her expression closed and cold. "I never understood what Finn saw in you."

"Where are you taking me?"

Jari nodded toward a bend in the river ahead. "You'll see soon enough. We're almost there."

The water swept them on and as they rounded the end of the gorge, the river opened out into a wider channel, slowing its pace to a lazy stream. Women gathered on the northern bank, slapping clothes on rocks as they hunkered down in groups, chatting as they worked. Children played in the shallows, the sun dappling their skin, droplets of water sparkling as they splashed each other. It could have been the Ganges in India or the Yangtze in China, or anywhere across either world where people lived near the banks of a river.

But as the water swept them on, the sound grew louder

from the bank — the noise of a huge population gathered in one place. The smell of burning rubbish and human waste overpowered the scent of blossom and as Jari paddled the boat toward the shallows, Sienna caught a glimpse of what lay beyond.

Rows of tents laid out in a grid system stretched as far as she could see. Hundreds of thousands of refugees crammed into a makeshift city. They escaped danger in their homelands only to be rejected by the countries they thought were safe haven. So they ended up here in the Borderlands.

Sienna frowned. The Shadow Cartographers and the Warlord's men were no kind-hearted saviors happy to provide refuge. So what were these people doing here?

The boat bumped up against the shoreline. Jari jumped out and dragged it further up the pebbled beach. She pulled a knife from her belt and bent to Sienna, holding the blade close to her throat.

"Don't try to run. There's no one to help you here." She slowly eased the knife down until it rested on the ropes that held Sienna. Jari cut through them and stepped back.

Sienna stood on wobbly legs and clambered from the boat. She reached back to touch the side of her head where pain still throbbed. Her hand came back red with blood from the open wound.

"You'll be fine." Jari nodded up the beach and slowly they walked up the bank.

A group of soldiers spotted them as they crested the top of the embankment, two of them with the half-moon tattoo of the Warlord. Jari raised a hand in the air as she came to stand next to Sienna, her own tattoo now their passport into the tent city.

As the soldiers approached, Jari pulled a coin from her pocket, a wolf's head imprinted on the side. The lead soldier looked surprised and his face shifted to one of respect, even a touch of fear.

Jari spun the coin between her fingers. "He's expecting me. Take us to him — now."

CHAPTER 19

Sienna followed Jari through the refugee camp flanked by soldiers on either side. There was no point trying to run, and even if she did manage to get away she'd soon be lost in this labyrinth. She glanced to either side as they walked. Groups of people sat around small fires, the scent of herbs mingling with smoke in the air as they brewed tea and cooked meager rations. The sound of coughing and crying came from inside the tents as they passed — children in distress or those who couldn't hold onto hope any longer. It was a desperate place filled with people on the edge of the abyss.

They turned into a causeway that ran the length of the camp with makeshift stalls and food vendors either side. People exchanged what little they had for a bowl of soup or another blanket. The refugees were thin, malnourished, and Sienna still couldn't work out why the Shadow Cartographers had herded them here. She knew of the mines on the edge of the Uncharted, a place where those who entered never returned, worked to death as they dug resources from the ground even as it shifted. But why were these people not taken there to work when they arrived over the border?

At the end of the causeway, a large tent stood in pride of place marked by the half-moon of the Warlord, surrounded by flaming torches. The soldiers marched toward it and despite the foreboding in her heart, Sienna went with them.

The flap of the tent opened as they approached and while several of the soldiers waited outside, two escorted her and Jari inside.

The tent was warm with braziers giving off heat and light around a large wooden table in the center. Platters of meat, fruit and fresh bread sat next to cups and a flagon of wine, the abundance all the more shocking next to the privations of the refugee camp. A man stood in front of the table, his back to them, wearing a cloak of wolf pelts around his broad shoulders.

Jari fell to her knees, head bent in respect. "I have the pieces of the map, my Lord."

The man turned, his rugged features criss-crossed with scars, his muscled frame taut and always ready for battle.

Kosai. Warlord of Old Aleppo. High Priest of Moloch, devourer of children — and Finn's father.

His piercing blue eyes met Sienna's as she stood, chin raised high. She would not kneel, not to him.

Sienna remembered Finn's words about his father's love of books, his staunch leadership in battle, his devotion to his soldiers. But all she could see was a man who had sent his daughter to the Fertility Halls to die in a bloody dungeon, her child cut from her belly.

Kosai laughed, his smile transforming his face into that of a handsome man. Sienna saw then where Finn had inherited his grace and perhaps even his charm.

He bent and lifted Jari's chin, raising her up to stand before him. "You bring me more than the map, I see." He nodded at Sienna. "Is she the one?"

"She can walk through maps, my Lord. I've even traveled with her." Jari pulled the pieces of the map from inside her jacket pocket and handed them to Kosai. "These are the fragments we found at the library, in the under-sea pyramid, and in the city of the air."

Kosai took them, his powerful hands holding them with the gentlest touch. He laid the three pieces on the wooden table, arranging them until it was clear where the final piece would fit.

"Finally, they are together once more." The cut-glass British accent came from behind her and Sienna turned to see Sir Douglas Mercator step into the tent.

He was a shade of the man who had entered her map shop not so long ago wanting to purchase her grandfather's legacy. His flesh hugged tight against his skull, his limbs were wasted, he looked as inconsequential as … a shadow.

Suddenly, Sienna realized the word was exactly right. This was what a Shadow Cartographer eventually became. Soon he would be only ethereal mist, magic with no physicality to hold it together, magic that became one with the Shadow itself.

"After more than six hundred years, the fragments of the map remain intact. And I have the final piece." Sir Douglas strode forward and it seemed to Sienna as if tendrils of shade writhed around his limbs as he moved.

He pulled a folded fragment from his pocket, and laid it on the desk with the others, unraveling and turning it until the edges matched up.

As he smoothed out the corners, Sienna sensed a tug from the map. A pulse ran through her veins, a quickening, an energy that drew her in. She took a step forward.

Sir Douglas beckoned her closer. "I know you're curious, Sienna. It calls to you, doesn't it? As every map calls to those with cartography in their blood."

Sienna couldn't speak, she could hardly breathe as she bent over the ancient skin reaching out for the lines etched upon it with gentle fingers. It depicted an island jungle ringed by jagged mountains to the coast, then hidden by miles of ocean, accessible only through this map. Trails criss-crossed the jungle centering on a habitation of sorts, perhaps a village, perhaps a city, it was unclear from the scale of the drawing how big it might be. The knights must have opened a portal and taken the worst of the infected through all those years ago. Perhaps the survivors lived on.

She noted a strange symbol on the side of the piece that Sir Douglas had retrieved, like an hourglass resting on its side. "What's that?"

"Time shifts in the Borderlands and even slows in parts of the Uncharted. This symbol indicates a place where time has slowed to almost nothing. It may have only been weeks since the knights left the island if there is anyone left to remember."

"How can that be?" Sienna shook her head. "It doesn't make sense. The knights would have wanted the plague to disappear completely, so why would they stop time when time itself could destroy it?"

"How do you know the knights wanted it gone for good?" Sir Douglas traced the symbol with one finger. "They were as much of the Shadow as they were of Earthside. Why do you think three of them ended up staying here, hiding their pieces of the map in the Borderlands? Perhaps they always knew it would be needed later."

"Needed for what?"

Sir Douglas shrugged. "What knights have always fought for. Kingdoms, justice … borders." He looked at her. "And now you will help me resurrect what they left behind."

Sienna shook her head. "I won't do it. You can kill me, sacrifice me to your bloodthirsty god. I don't care. But I won't travel through that map. I won't bring back the plague."

Sir Douglas arched one perfect eyebrow. "Not even to save your precious friends?"

"What do you mean?" Sienna stammered. "You know where Mila and Perry are?" Her eyes darted to Kosai. "And Finn?"

The Warlord laughed. "My errant son comes for you, despite knowing the fate that awaits him. His die is cast, but the other two." He shrugged. "They're on the river heading here right now. My scouts along the bank follow their every move. You can still save them."

Sir Douglas put his hand on Sienna's arm, his bony fingers a freezing imprint on her skin. "Give in to your curiosity. Be the Mapwalker I know you are. Go to the island, see what is left of the plague and bring us back something that will save your friends."

"But what if I get attacked, what if I die of the plague?"

"Oh, don't worry. You won't be going alone." Sir Douglas beckoned to the entrance of the tent.

Sienna turned, her eyes widening as she saw who it was.

* * *

Mila and Perry stood with Finn looking down at the refugee camp. Rows of tents stretched into the distance, the glow of tiny fires interspersing the darkness as cries of children mingled with the barking of dogs and the sound of a fiddle. Music brought hope no matter how dark the night and somewhere down there, someone still believed in a future.

They had traveled by day on the river, propelled by the current and Mila's magic pushing them ever faster but now it looked as if finding Sienna in this labyrinth would be almost impossible.

Perry gazed out at the tent city. "How many people do you think there are down there?"

Finn's expression hardened. "I've heard this camp has over one hundred thousand, and the same again by the western gate, with rumors of more camps." He spun to face Perry. "These people are only here because they were rejected from Earthside. They fled their own cities for fear of being slaughtered and you turned them away at your borders. It's the fault of your kind that they are here."

Perry nodded. "You're right, but our people were just protecting their homes, their way of life."

Finn looked out again, his face wistful. "All these people want is to go home. They don't want your way of life. They want their own."

"And they'll do anything to get it back," Mila whispered, sudden realization dawning as she looked out at the tent city crammed full of refugees who only had one goal.

She spun around and grabbed Finn's arm. "You mentioned more camps by the other gates back into Earthside, right?"

Finn nodded. "Yes, there could be as many as fifteen more, all stationed at portal crossing points. But the gates are closed."

"For now," Perry stated. "But if all the gates are opened at the same time, these people will swarm through, desperate to get to their homes again."

"It's more than that," Mila said. "Disease doesn't respect borders. You can't reason with it, you can't pen it up in a refugee camp and banish it from your land." She swept her arm out over the camp, taking in the expanse of people below. "This is why the Shadow Cartographers want the Map of Plagues. These people are the invasion. When the gates open, they will stream back over, infected with the plague. The numbers will overwhelm Earthside cities, especially if they're all released at the same time."

Perry looked aghast. "It will devastate Earthside and there will be few left who could stop the borders shifting further after that."

Mila nodded. "The Shadow Cartographers will get their land back, but at what cost?"

Finn sighed. "You don't get it. They don't care for you. They will wipe you out as your people used disease to wipe out those conquered before you. Aboriginal Australians, Native Americans, African nations. The remnant of those people are here with a cultural memory of genocide bestowed on their ancestors. Do you think they care if Earthside is devastated by plague now?"

Mila reached for his hand. "Do *you* care, Finn? You've seen where we come from, you stood in The Circus and we fought your father together for the ordinary people in the streets of Earthside. Will you fight with us now?"

Finn pointed to the tents below. "I'll fight for them."

"We still have time," Perry said. "The Shadow Cartographers won't send people through the portals until they're infected. And they won't risk releasing bubonic plague through the gates. It won't spread fast enough. It has to go pneumonic and it takes time to infect the lungs and go airborne."

Finn shook his head. "You're in the Borderlands now and everything changes when it crosses over from your world. Don't think you know this plague anymore. It may have mutated into something new. We have to find Sienna before it's too late."

CHAPTER 20

XANDER STEPPED THROUGH THE doorway, his dark mop of loose curls longer now, a short beard outlining his jaw. His hazel-green eyes gazed at her with a touch of his old languid self but Sienna could see lines at the corners of his full mouth and he had an air of exhaustion, as if he had been draining his magic too fast. He had given up everything on Earthside to be here, but it didn't look like Xander was thriving in the Borderlands.

"It's about time we traveled together again," he said, his wry smile reminding her of old times.

Sienna pointedly turned her back on him and looked at Sir Douglas. "Why him?"

"His magic is useful and his lion will protect you both." He looked at his watch. "Besides, you know each other well enough to deal with whatever you find and he will bring us back the samples we need. Now, it's time to go."

Sienna took a deep breath as her mind whirled with possibilities. There was nowhere to run and if she refused, her friends would die. She knew what the Warlord was capable of and it seemed Sir Douglas was more shadow than man now. There would be no mercy.

Then there was the map itself. It pulled her in, she felt its tug deep inside like an undertow that threatened to drag her down to the depths. It whispered of mystery and secrets revealed after hundreds of years, secrets the knights had died to protect. She wanted to know where it led to.

"I'll go but I need your word that my friends won't be harmed."

The Warlord nodded. Sir Douglas waved his hand as if swatting a fly. "Of course. They mean nothing. Now, go."

Sienna stepped closer to the map, placing her hand over the center where the four pieces joined. She held out her other hand for Xander. His palm was warm, his fingers strong as they wrapped around hers.

She closed her eyes and dived into the map. At first the sensation of flying made her heart soar with joy. This was where she felt free, in this place between the pages of the world — but then the air grew chill and a dense mist swirled around her. Strange sounds came from the eddies of cloud, the crackling of burnt skin, the low moans of an animal in pain. Sienna hoped that the mist stayed around them. She didn't want to see what lay beyond.

She tried to travel faster but Xander's weight lay heavy on her. Even though his betrayal still stung, she would not let him go. She would not abandon him in this in-between world.

The plague island must be below them now and in her mind, Sienna imagined the hourglass tipping, the sand running out. She surfed down upon the grains, descending through the clouds.

They parted and there it was. The island, dense with jungle, the city at its heart hemmed in by jagged mountains. And it was a city, at least the size of one, albeit without the grand structures of Earthside or even the ramshackle growth of a long-term settlement. But as Sienna descended, she realized it was silent. There were no people in the streets, no animals wandering around. Even the surrounding jungle was quiet.

Could Sir Douglas have been wrong about the meaning of the hourglass? Were they six hundred years too late to find any evidence of the plague?

She chose a landing place in the middle of what looked like a public square, a clearing surrounded by stone buildings. One was larger than the rest, marked with a cross.

Xander rolled to his hands and knees, coughing and retching as his body adapted to the strange journey.

"That was awful," he groaned. "Now I remember why I never wanted to do that again."

"Happy to leave you here when I go back." Sienna scanned the hushed buildings with a sense that something was out there watching. "Get up quickly. We need to get out of the open."

She looked up at the church. Something about it drew her in. It was a simple structure but the stones of its walls had been selected and placed with care. It was testament to human faith that even at the end of the world, some could still look for God. Sienna hoped they had found him even here.

She walked toward the door, carved from what looked like dark oily wood from the surrounding jungle. As she approached, the smell of decay rose up around her. She stumbled back, hand to her face.

"What is it?" Xander stood to his feet, a little unsteady at first but soon gaining strength.

"In there." She pointed at the church. "I think we're too late."

* * *

Xander followed Sienna's gaze to the church, the cross on its wall a reminder of the simple country chapels in the Cotswolds near his home. No, he couldn't think of it as home anymore. That was Earthside, a land stolen from those he now served. He sighed. Perhaps Sienna should leave him here. Life might be simpler.

He walked toward the door, the stench rising as he drew closer. He pinched his nose and tried to breathe in a shallow manner, his heart pounding as he pushed at the entrance-way. The door was jammed, something pressing against it from inside.

"Hello, is anyone there?" But even as Xander called out, he knew there was nothing alive inside the church.

He thrust his shoulder against the door. A crack rang out and he fell inward. A broken plank lay on the floor as if someone had forced it against the door, a barrier against what lay beyond.

Xander stepped inside, Sienna close behind. He heard her gasp as he tried to process the scene.

A huge pile of bodies stacked against the walls, as high as the church itself and several rows deep. In front of them, two men and a woman lay curled together. They must have been the last to die as the plague ravaged the place. It couldn't have been that long ago because decomposition was still in process. Time must have shifted here as Sir Douglas promised but Xander doubted if there would be anything he could take back as evidence of the plague. He grimaced as he looked at the bodies. He really didn't want to lug one of those back.

He turned around slowly to examine the church itself. Why had they holed up in here? They should have buried those bodies in the jungle, away from the rest of the popula-tion. Some of them might have made it if they hadn't kept the disease so close.

"Xander!"

He spun around to see Sienna desperately trying to shut the door, leaning her weight against it. He ran back to help her push — and caught a glimpse through a crack to the outside.

A sea of rats, overgrown and mutated, snarling with teeth bared, their silent surge a perversion of natural behavior. Somehow this island had turned the rats into the dominant predator, destroying the population with plague and presumably devouring any bodies left outside until there was nothing left to eat.

Until fresh blood arrived just minutes ago.

Xander shuddered and thrust the door closed. He and Sienna sank to the ground, their backs against the door as the rodents scratched and banged their heads against the wood. The pile of rotting corpses loomed ahead and Xander wondered whether taking a body would be a better idea than trying to wrestle one of those rats back to the camp.

"What now?" Sienna asked, her face pale as she looked up at him. "I can get us back out of here as soon as you're ready to go."

Xander shook his head, imagining his fate — and Sienna's — if he returned with empty hands. "I can't go back without a sample." He pulled two waterproof sacks out of his jacket pocket. "Sir Douglas gave me these. If we can get a rat and — something — from that pile, then we can go."

He edged away from the door, keeping pressure on it with one hand while reaching for the broken plank with the other. "We just need to block this shut while we figure everything out."

Xander hooked the plank and used it to pull one of the old pews closer, blocking the entranceway with its weight. "That will hold them at bay for a little while."

Sienna touched his hand, her eyes soft. "What happened, Xander? Why betray us back in the castle that day? Why work for the Shadow side?"

Her words echoed deep inside him and for a moment, he wondered whether she might help him return to his old life. He shook his head and gave a wry smile. "You haven't been working with the Ministry long. You don't know how little we're allowed to use our magic. They're more concerned with protecting those on Earthside from the knowledge of what lies beyond the border. Hell, most don't even know the Borderlands exist."

He stood up and pulled the ragged leather scrap from his pocket, his creatures etched around the edges. "I felt like half of me was trapped inside, and over here, despite the difficulties, I can be myself. I can do what I was born to do. I am an Illustrator."

Xander threw the leather on the floor and Asada, his lion, stepped out, shaking his magnificent mane. The beast nuzzled into Xander and then turned to look at Sienna, golden eyes acknowledging her presence.

"He's part of me," Xander said. "I understand that now. Asada is not some separate being that I conjure from the edges of the map, but an extension of my magic. Back on Earthside, it was like I functioned underwater, hardly able to move at all. But here, I'm free." He sighed. "Do you understand what I mean?"

To his surprise, Sienna nodded. "I can't say anything to the others but when I'm between the lines of the map, when I travel, I hear a whisper that I want to follow. The Shadow calls to me, Xander, and part of me wants to give in."

Xander couldn't believe what he heard and all at once, possibilities tumbled through his mind. "If you want to stay here, then there's hope, can you see that? You're powerful, Sienna. We could join the Resistance together, we could change things here in the Borderlands. Really change them, not just use all our energy trying to get back land on Earthside. We could make a new start."

Sienna gave a shy smile. "I could be with Finn. Be part of building a new way of life here, just as I promised."

Xander laughed. "Whatever you want. It's all possible now." A screech of wood on stone came from the door as the scratching and squeaking of rats grew louder. "Well, it's all possible once we get out of here."

"What about the plague?" Sienna said. "We have to take back samples and I can't leave Mila, Perry and Finn at the Warlord's mercy."

Xander took her hand. "We'll figure that out once we get back there. We have each other now."

She smiled. "Okay, let's do it." She grabbed one of the waterproof bags and looked at the pile of corpses, her face a mask of revulsion. "Which one of these do we take?"

Xander steeled himself and walked over to the pile of corpses — old men, young women, children, even babies, all lying together, equal in death.

One of the babies caught his eye, black lumps under its arms with grey veins spreading out like a sunburst of ash.

Sienna followed his gaze. "Oh no. You can't be serious?"

Xander raised the bag. "It fits." He pulled the bloated corpse from the pile, turning his face away as the stench rose up, making him gag. His stomach twitched and he almost hurled but he managed to hold it in. Sienna helped him close the bag, her face twisted in revulsion. Then together, they turned back toward the door.

"Maybe we can open it a little, let one in, then bag it quickly?"

Xander shrugged. "I don't have any other ideas."

They positioned themselves behind the door with Asada standing in the center of the room. He growled and pawed at the floor, ready to fight.

"Just pin it, boy, don't kill it," Xander called back, sensing the lion's understanding. He looked at Sienna. "Ready?"

"As I'll ever be."

Xander pulled the pew back a little and inched the door open. A thick grey muzzle pushed against the gap, nose sniffing the air, whiskers twitching. He let out the door a little more.

As the smell of the dead wafted out, the rats went wild, screeching and clambering over one another to try and reach the door. The swarm pushed forward, beady eyes fixed on the pile of corpses as they forced their way into the chapel.

Sienna fell backward as the mass of grey bodies surged in and Xander couldn't hold it alone. The door gaped open and a flurry of rodents raced inside.

"Quick, stop them!" Xander pushed hard against the door, Sienna rolled back to join him and they managed to get it closed again.

But it was too late.

Six of the giant mutated rats had made it inside. The creatures dashed toward the dead, thrusting their heads into the pile of bodies, the crack of bones filling the air as the stench intensified.

Sienna and Xander sat with their backs against the door, frozen still. Xander held a palm out to Asada to try and keep him calm — but the lion couldn't help his animal nature.

He swiped at one of the rats, batting it sideways then lunging to rip at its neck, shaking the beast in his jaws until its squeaking stopped.

The others turned from the pile of the dead, black beady eyes assessing the scene. Xander could almost sense their excitement as they spied fresh meat.

CHAPTER 21

As the rats began to advance on their prey, Sienna picked up one of the huge Bibles from the back of the pew, handing another to Xander. They moved slowly, eyes fixed on the rodents. Xander could see the individual hairs on one of the rats as it drew closer, each as thick and spiny as a porcupine quill. It bared its teeth ready to charge.

Asada pounced from behind, his huge legs crushing the beast's back with a crunch.

The other rats attacked.

One rodent dashed toward Sienna, its yellow teeth in a grimace, its thick pink tail lashing behind. She stood, brandishing the Bible like a baseball bat. It was almost upon her when she swung the heavy book, thwacking the beast on the side of its head, knocking it into the wall. She followed it down, beating it with the Lord's book, while she screamed her anger.

Xander turned as three giant rats lunged at Asada.

He swiped at one, knocking it into the wall, but another jumped on the lion's back, worrying at his neck. The last latched its teeth onto his forelegs, biting down and shaking its head to dig deeper.

Blood welled and Asada roared, ripping the rat from his leg, crunching it between his jaws before spitting it to the ground, a broken husk.

Xander swung the great Bible at the rat on the lion's back, connecting with a dull thud and knocking the creature to the floor. It writhed, spine broken, mewling with pain.

Asada suddenly dropped to his haunches, licking his foreleg as a black stain spread across the limb from the bite mark. Xander rushed to his side, his arms around the great mane. "Hold on. You're going to be alright, boy. I promise."

But even as he spoke, Xander saw a mark appear on his own arm. A sudden pain lanced through him as the black spread over Asada's skin and his own flesh.

Xander looked at Sienna. "I can feel it in my veins." His voice broke as he tried to hold back tears. "The plague has mutated. It's fast moving now."

He leaned against Asada, sensing the lion's strength falter even as his own began to fade.

* * *

Sienna quickly looked around for anything she could use to slow the disease. She pulled a shirt from one of the bodies and tied it as tight as she could around Xander's arm above the spreading black. Maybe the tourniquet would slow the movement of poison.

She thought about doing the same to Asada but he growled softly as he sank his huge head onto his paws, nuzzling against Xander. The lion might be an extension of Xander somehow, but he was still a wild animal. She needed to get them both out of here.

Sienna picked up the remaining sack and gingerly pushed the mewling rat into it, avoiding the jaws with those lethal teeth. She gathered up the other bag with its gruesome contents then pulled the ritual knife from inside her jacket. She nicked the side of her palm and as her blood dripped on the floor, mingling with Asada's, she hesitated.

She could take Xander and Asada straight back to the Ministry. He would have a chance at surviving and the Borderlanders would not have the plague.

But then she thought of Mila and Perry — and Finn. Their survival depended on her returning with the samples.

She sighed. Who's to say what the Ministry would do with the plague anyway? Since discovering the Mapwalkers, she had been torn as to who was right about the border, whose side she should fight on, or whether there could be any resolution to the question of who the land belonged to. Would those on Earthside be any better if they were handed this biological weapon?

She trusted her friends and together, they would figure out the next step.

Sienna drew a map with the scarlet drops, a map of a refugee camp with a grand tent at its center marked with the head of a wolf. She closed her eyes and traveled through.

* * *

When the smell of woodsmoke overpowered the stench of the bloated dead, Sienna opened her eyes. Xander and Asada lay before her, both unconscious, the two sacks by her side, one moving as the dying rat shifted inside.

Sir Douglas stood over her with a triumphant smile. He clicked his fingers at the guards on the door. "Bring the stretchers. We need to transport them to the pens."

His words echoed through Sienna's mind as she struggled to get her bearings. She was still woozy from traveling so fast, carrying the weight of the sick and the dying, the heavy load of the plague virus dragging her down in some unknown way. She couldn't stand up, she could barely breathe properly.

Sir Douglas ignored her as he opened the two sacks, his smile widening at what lay within.

The Warlord, Kosai, peered in at the rat, his nose wrinkling at the smell. "I'm getting my men out of here before you release those creatures into the camp."

Sir Douglas nodded. "Go now, take your best soldiers and start incursions into Earthside. Be ready when I open the gates fully." He laughed and shook his head. "They won't know what's coming until it's too late."

Sienna thought of her father and Bridget back in Bath. She needed to warn them of what was coming but she could barely move, let alone get herself and the others out of there. Her limbs felt weighed down as if she was smothered under a thick blanket and she could almost feel the spread of shadow in her veins.

A group of soldiers stepped into the tent and bundled them all onto stretchers, tying them down with strips of cloth. Xander and Asada didn't surface from oblivion as they were manhandled. Sienna tried to resist, but she was helpless against the strength of the men. She gave up, pretending to be woozy even as she began to feel her mind return to its former sharpness. Where were Mila, Perry and Finn?

The soldiers carried the stretchers double time back down the causeway toward a row of tents at the bottom of the hill nearer the river. As they approached, the stink of animal bodies grew stronger and Sienna heard the sound of squeaking — just like the plague island.

More rats. And they sounded hungry.

The soldiers carried the stretchers inside one of the biggest tents and laid them down on a dais in the middle of a series of pens each containing hundreds of rats trapped in wooden crates. Sienna tried to calculate how many there were in the tent and then multiplied it by the other similar tents nearby. There must be tens of thousands of the creatures. But how would they all be infected?

Sir Douglas stalked into the tent, his presence even more

spectral than it had been before. A young woman with short silver hair skipped along by his side, her face angelic but something about her made Sienna's skin crawl and her blood turn to ice. She feigned exhaustion, relaxing her body as if still semi-conscious even as she wanted to cry out in fear.

They approached the dais and the young woman ran to Asada, her slender fingers stroking the lion's fur. She bit her lip and clenched her fists with excitement. "This one first."

Sir Douglas nodded. "Of course, Elf." He waved across the sea of rats. "You know what to do."

The girl placed her hand on the lion's flank and stretched out the other over the first pen of rodents. Her body tensed and then an almost ecstatic look came over her face, as if she was touched by some unseen force. The rats squeaked wildly as Asada's body began to wither, his muscles dissolving under his tawny skin. Xander moaned and writhed on his stretcher, still unconscious but deeply connected to his lion through the magic that bound them together.

"No!" Sienna couldn't help herself. "Stop it. You're killing him."

Elf looked down at her with eyes like a pool of ice. There was no regard for life in those depths, no love for her fellow creatures, just pure joy at the thrill of power that ran through her veins.

Sienna knew then that she had tasted a glimmer of that joy when she traveled and if she gave in to it, she would be like Elf, a creature completely of the shadow.

Asada's body deflated, a bag of skin with dead bone inside, his life force and the plague that infected him now within the rats in the pen before them.

Sir Douglas gestured to a group of soldiers. "Take those crates to the other camps at the far gates and release them there. Be ready for the Warlord's signal."

The soldiers raced forward, lifted the crates and headed out the door. Sienna watched them go, dread rising within her at what they planned.

Elf walked to Xander's side and looked down on the young man. She stroked the hair from his pale face, sweating now as the black nodules of plague covered both arms and rose up his neck. "He must have been beautiful once," she whispered.

"Please, help him," Sienna sobbed.

Elf placed her hand on Xander's chest and stretched out the other over the next pen of rats. Her body tensed again as dark power surged through her. Xander convulsed under her touch, his body withering as the life was sucked from him.

Sienna wept for her friend's passing.

It was only a matter of minutes to reduce another life to dust and Elf seemed to grow in stature as she radiated the plague out to the rats gathered below. Another phalanx of soldiers picked up the next set of crates and ran with them into the night.

Then Elf turned to look at Sienna, her eyes alive with blue fire as she assessed her next victim.

CHAPTER 22

SIR DOUGLAS STEPPED IN front of Sienna, arms stretched wide to protect his possession. "Not this one. She's a Blood Mapwalker and she's not infected anyway." He gestured at the sacks. "There are diseased remains in there. Use those for the rest."

Elf stared back, challenging him, raising her hands as if she would use them against even her own. Sienna recognized that she was on the edge of her control and yet her power was barely yet grown. It was terrifying in one so young. If these were the children of the Shadow Cartographers, the future would bring far more terrors than the Ministry realized.

If there was a future after the plague of rats had stormed the gates into Earthside, of course.

Sir Douglas opened his palm and curled a pillar of flame into the air, spinning it into shapes of sharp-toothed rodents feeding on bloated corpses. Elf smiled at the fiery tableau and took a step back, acknowledging his superior power — at least for now. He had some kind of hold over her, Sienna realized, and as she looked closer, she saw a faint resemblance between them. The patrician nose, even the arrogant stance. Could Elf be Sir Douglas's daughter — and Perry's sister?

* * *

Perry watched in horror as a boiling mass of rats streamed out of white tents at the bottom of the hill. From their vantage point high on the hill, he could see the bristly bodies writhing as they fought to find a way out of the pack and into the wider camp. The high-pitched squeaking was soon drowned out by the sound of screams.

The sound of drums beating suddenly echoed across the camp, slow at first but with a rising tempo.

"My father's war drums," Finn said, looking out to the source of the sound. "They must be about to open the gate and let those people through along with the plague. We have to stop them."

Mila pointed at the soldiers herding people forward. "There are too many, and you said there were other gates, too." She shook her head. "We have to find Sienna. We have to get back to Earthside and close the gates from the inside."

* * *

In the tent of rats, Sir Douglas untied Sienna from the stretcher and pulled her to her feet. "Don't fight me now," he whispered. "Leave Elf to her magic before she turns it on you."

Sienna nodded her agreement but he did not let her wrist go as they walked to the door, his bony fingers tight and cold against her skin. With every step, Sienna expected the sudden wrench of magic draining her life energy but it never came and when they stepped out into the night air, she found herself almost breathless with relief.

Then the sound of squealing rats and crying children surrounded her, the shouts of people trying to fight the creatures and the screams of those bitten and infected.

"How can you do this?" Sienna whispered. "These people came to you for help."

Sir Douglas dragged her up the hill back to the main tent, his hand like a vise around her wrist. "These are your people, not mine. Their fate is the fault of Earthside and their death will be the instrument of justice."

They reached the tent, guarded by two soldiers who held their ground even as mayhem broke out around them. Their eyes were wide with fear but they stood to attention as Sir Douglas approached. He pushed Sienna forward and followed her in.

"There is one more thing I must do tonight. You'll stay here for now, but after this is over, you'll return with me to the tower in the Castle of the Shadow."

Sienna gasped as the vision of the turrets came to her mind, the place that called to her when she traveled. It promised dark joy, a sense of purpose, a future where she could live within her magic.

But that was also the training ground for Elf and those of her kind.

Sienna shook her head. "Never."

Sir Douglas smiled and opened his palm. This time, instead of flame, he conjured a ball of shadow, its surface like the shimmering waters of a deep pool. There were creatures inside, flying through the pearly depths with wings of gossamer.

"You'll change your mind once you see the possibilities." Sir Douglas let the ball go and it floated toward Sienna. She reached out a hand in wonder to touch it and as she did, the orb turned ashen and grew bigger until it surrounded her with a bubble of silver shadow.

She fought its power but her shouts were like those in a tomb, echoing back to her, bouncing off the walls of her shadow prison. She couldn't hear the screams of the infected now, she could only hear her own heartbeat. The creatures flying in the clouds drew closer until she could see their teeth and feel their claws. Sienna fell to the ground, hands wrapped around her head as they attacked.

* * *

Sir Douglas watched Sienna curl up within her shadowed cocoon. The creatures were all in her mind, but the torture would keep her occupied while he completed his own mission.

This was the last time he would have to cross over, the Shadow had promised him that, but it was critical to the success of the plan. He sighed. The mission was dangerous and somewhere deep inside, the part of him that was still a man wondered if it was the right choice. Then the Shadow rose within him, darkness suffusing his blood. He gasped as a thousand thousand pinpricks of shade pierced his heart, shuddering as the ecstasy of pain and pleasure possessed him.

As the convulsions passed, Sir Douglas strode out of the tent toward the gate, his eyes dark with shadow, his skin more shade than flesh. It was time for the reckoning.

* * *

Deep within the Ministry of Maps below Bath Abbey, the Illuminated Cartographer sensed the borders shift, then he heard the blaring alarm that warned of a breach. The sounds of the Mapwalker team running for the War Room echoed through the corridors beyond, a flurry of activity that seemed ever more frequent these days.

He stirred in his nest of maps, the rustling around him intensified by his movement. His own heartbeat pulsed ink through the living borders, but he was old and it was weaker now, the ink thinner in his veins, the magic diminished by his own fragility.

The library was bright with rays from the moon. Even though it was deep beneath the earth, a series of mirrors reflected light down into the darkest corners. A sheen of pale blue spread across the piles of maps, some rolled and stacked, others spilling over buried furniture. It smelled of rosewater, spice and incense, reminiscent of the souk in Istanbul where cultures crossed in an ever-moving melting pot. This was his home. Once upon a time, he had known where to find every map, he could summon the details of each drawing, each line, but now memory slipped away like the moonlight shifting with every passing minute.

The sound of shouting came from the corridors beyond, the clash of steel, a moan of pain. Then footsteps coming to his door.

The Illuminated Cartographer shifted his great bulk behind one of the giant bookcases, pulling the maps about him, their spiraling mass keeping him hidden in a pile of contours and symbols of the land.

The door burst open.

Two huge Feral Borderlanders stalked in, faces marked by the half-moon, sharp swords clenched in meaty fists. They stood either side of the door as Sir Douglas Mercator walked through, his aristocratic features more wolf-like than human now, his skin etched with shadow, his eyes as dark as the void.

The Illuminated Cartographer gathered his maps closer still, winding them about his body, protecting his heart with their pages. They would protect him for a while, but even as death stalked him in this realm, he could feel every hammering blow against the many gates of the border. His weakness was more than physical now and it threatened all of Earthside.

"It's time," Sir Douglas said softly, his voice as cold and

sharp as a blade. "You have sought peace all these years and now I will give it to you. But no one said peace would be on your terms." He raised his arms and opened his hands, conjuring balls of fire. The heat of the center burned blue surrounded by a penumbra of bright orange, its edges the scarlet red of blood.

The Illuminated Cartographer shrank back from the flame, every fiber of his entwined being recoiling from the element of destruction.

"You can't burn this place," the Illuminated Cartographer called out. "It's the beating heart of the maps. The borders will crumble if they are all destroyed. The ancient magic will dissolve and there will be nothing holding the two worlds apart."

"Exactly." Sir Douglas hurled the balls of flame into the thickest part of the pile of maps. The dry paper caught and the fire spread quickly even as Sir Douglas cast more heat into the blaze, his face alive with power.

Agony seared through the Illuminated Cartographer as he reeled back from the burning bookcase, pain suffusing his body even as the fire devoured the maps, each page like a piece of his own flesh. He wept for the destruction in the library even as he desperately tried to keep the border intact between the worlds.

One of the bookcases crashed to the floor, sending up a plume of sparks before spreading the fire further into the library. Sir Douglas laughed with the mania of destruction as he burned the ancient maps, pieces of ash rising in the updraft, whirling in the flame.

The Illuminated Cartographer crawled deeper into his warren of burning paper, coughing and retching as he struggled to breathe. He didn't have much time. He could sense the holes in the borders widening, the gates pushed open, every second weakening what remained of the ancient magic.

It was almost too late.

CHAPTER 23

The sound of fighting came from the corridor beyond and this time, gunshots. As the two Feral Borderlanders ran out of the room, Sir Douglas lowered his hands.

"Give up now and I'll spare this city the worst of the plague."

The Illuminated Cartographer remained silent as he gathered the last of his strength, tugging on ancient pathways that wound through the maps and into his veins. He pulled the vellum closer, huddling deeper inside layers of projection and elevation. Smoke enveloped the library now, the smell of burning like a pyre of the damned.

In the corner, a painted celestial globe mounted on wooden legs sat just out of reach of the fire, behind the line of Sir Douglas's sight. The Illuminated Cartographer sent his magic out through the tangle of maps, reaching crumpled paper tendrils out to grasp and wrap around the legs.

Sir Douglas raised his hands again. "So be it." He unleashed a hail of fire that swept over the remaining maps, his face transformed by the leaping flames.

As the lick of extreme heat reached the Illuminated Cartographer, he curled his hands and lifted the globe with the edges of his magic, wielding it as a giant club to beat at his enemy.

Sir Douglas fell to the floor under the weight of the globe, his fire extinguished as he smashed his head on the ground.

Then he rolled free, dark blood dripping from his forehead, face distorted by fury. He kicked the globe away and directed his stream of flame at what remained of the twisted paper.

Then he turned back to the remains of the library. "That will be the end of you."

He raised his hands once more.

The door burst open and the two Feral Borderlander guards stumbled in, bleeding from multiple wounds as they fought the Mapwalkers who chased them. Sir Douglas spun around, backing away into the flaming library. His little team was outnumbered but they had achieved their purpose. This place was finished.

The Illuminated Cartographer sensed the truth of it and as his vision blurred with smoke and ash, he saw Sir Douglas leave his guards to their death and dart out the back of the library toward a door that led to the Gallery of Geographical Maps where he could slip back into the Borderlands. No doubt he would return with an invading force through the holes in the border.

The future rose before the Illuminated Cartographer's eyes, a vision of plague devastation and a land laid waste before the Shadow claimed it in an orgy of destruction.

There was only one way to stop it, but he didn't have the strength left. After so many generations, he had failed Earthside. He closed his eyes, tears of ink rolling down his cheeks, as the darkness overtook him.

* * *

Bridget let the Mapwalker team subdue the Borderlander soldiers before she entered the library. John Farren limped in alongside her, his bleak expression matching her own. He reached for her hand and they stood for a minute, taking in the ruined desolation, words failing them both.

Sir Douglas had almost destroyed the library and then escaped in the smoke and chaos, but perhaps there was still a glimmer of hope.

"He has to be in here somewhere." Bridget put her sleeve over her mouth and pulled out her torch as John did the same. They began sweeping the wreckage for the Illuminated Cartographer.

He couldn't be dead yet or they would be overrun with invading Borderlanders, but he must be deeply wounded. The monitoring systems were in meltdown in the War Room, alarms blaring from gates all over the world as the border weakened. Few understood that the blood magic of this one man maintained the borders, a secret handed down to only a few over the hundreds of years of the Ministry's existence.

Even fewer understood that this was still the same man who had dwelled within the library for hundreds of years, his own longevity bound up in the long life of the maps around him, a mutual preservation of creator and created. Some annals said that the origin of the Shadow was a family feud that left twin brothers on either side of the border. Whatever the truth, no one had ever thought the Illuminated Cartographer could be laid low this way.

But the world had changed.

In her lifetime, Bridget had seen the Borderlanders go from being a ragtag bunch of mercenaries with occasional incursions into their world, to detailed invasion plans to retake what they saw as their lands on Earthside. Their magic grew stronger with their aggressive breeding programs while those on this side of the border only weakened as bloodlines were lost. Now it seemed like the Shadow Cartographers had the upper hand.

Tears welled as Bridget surveyed the destruction in front of her, piles of ash where once precious manuscripts lay, smoldering remains of vellum masterpieces, maps of places that had been lost over the years, places they could never find again now.

In the corner, she noticed a bigger pile, the outer layers burned but inside there might be a hollow of protection.

"Over here!" she called out.

John rushed over and together they pulled off the outer layers of maps until the body of the old man lay curled in what remained of his cocoon. His face was covered with ash, his skin no longer pulsing with the dark ink that sustained the magic of the Ministry.

Bridget's heart pounded with fear as she looked down at him. It was over, it had to be. She imagined the borders crumbling and Borderlanders streaming through as they knelt here in the remains of a once great place.

Then his eyes flickered and opened.

Bridget looked down and saw a world of star maps within them, a kaleidoscope of deep blue sky filled with possible futures.

He lifted one hand, the map fragments around him curling with his movement, wrapping themselves around Bridget's wrist. She felt his pulse — faint, but still there.

"You are the only hope now," he whispered. "I am finished but you're young and vibrant. You must be the new Illuminated Cartographer."

Bridget's eyes widened at his words. Fresh blood poured into the veins of the maps would strengthen the border and renew the power of the Ministry, but she had never considered that she might be the source. She looked around the burnt library, the broken shelves, the devastation of the place. If she took his mantle, she would have to stay here until her own lifespan ended. She would never walk in the sun again, never have the freedom to roam.

John reached out a hand to cup her cheek. "You don't have to do this, Bridget. Think of all you would have to give up. There must be another way."

In his eyes, Bridget saw a future filled with love, a second chance for them both. But if the borders failed, there would be little future for any of them.

"You … must … choose," the Illuminated Cartographer said as his eyes flickered closed once more. As Bridget felt his pulse fade, she knew she was out of time.

* * *

Mila led the others down the hill, her pace quickening until they reached the edge of the terrified crowds. As the rats spread out from the main tent, people tried to flee but the Warlord's soldiers blocked the perimeter, keeping the masses within the camp. Sounds of screams and shouts filled the air as parents gathered children into their arms, climbing where they could to get away from the rats but the relentless horde infiltrated even the furthest corners.

A river of rodents flowed up the hill toward them. There was no time to go around.

Mila heard the metal slide of Finn drawing his sword, the whoosh of Perry's flame. She reached out to the sense of water around her, pulling it from barrels and troughs nearby, curling it into spinning whips of shining droplets. They strode through the horde of creatures, cutting and burning, whipping them away.

But those around them were not so lucky.

A man cowered against a tent pole as they passed. Mila saw a rat sink its teeth into his flesh and watched in horror as the man's skin quickly turned mottled shades of blue and black. This was no longer any kind of plague seen before in the history of humanity. This was a Shadow plague now, hybrid death magic, fast and unstoppable. It would decimate Earthside and there was only a faint hope to hold it back now.

The border that had held for so many generations weakened as the seconds passed, she could feel it in the way her magic called to her darker self. Mila understood that if they were trapped here, she would lose herself in this midnight realm. She thought of Zippy, his happy spaniel face snuffling in the reeds at the edge of the canal. She conjured home to her mind, birdsong in the trees above the waters, the cheep of ducklings in spring, the smell of woodsmoke from the canal boats. All threatened by this invasion.

Mila started to run, suddenly aware of the sands of time rushing through the hourglass ever faster. Perry and Finn ran with her, the three of them racing toward the grand tent at the center of the causeway.

Two soldiers stood outside, distracted by the craziness around them and Finn despatched one with a few cuts of his blade and knocked the other out with the pommel of his sword.

They raced into the tent.

"Sienna!" Mila shouted, looking around in desperation for her friend.

There was a shape on the floor wrapped in spun silver like a giant cocoon. The surface was opaque, like clouds scudding across a stormy sky. Mila frowned and then realization rose within her, certainty of what — of who — lay within.

"What have they done to you?" Mila fell to her knees next to the cocoon, reaching out a hand to press through the surface.

Perry snatched her hand away. "Don't touch it. It's shadow-weave and it'll stick to your skin, too. You'll end up in there with her." Mila looked up in surprise at his knowledge. Perry shrugged. "It's one of my father's favorite tricks. He used to punish me with it back when I was young." His eyes darkened with the memory.

Finn walked around Sienna's encased form, frowning as he tried to find an opening, anything to lever his way inside. "How do we get her out?"

Perry smiled. "The shadow-weave needs form to cluster around. I think we might have a volunteer."

He darted outside and dragged in the body of the soldier that Finn had knocked unconscious, moving it close to Sienna's cocoon. He pushed the soldier's leg with his own, careful not to touch the shadow-weave as the man's limb sank inside the grey. Spindles of weave reached out, moving up the limb as it crawled over the soldier's body, receding a little from Sienna, leaving one of her arms outside its orbit.

Finn grasped her wrist and slowly pulled her body further away as the shadow-weave settled over the soldier until Sienna was finally free.

Her eyes were closed, her breathing shallow and Mila could see dark curls of shadow beneath her pale skin. She had used her magic too much recently. Could her blood be polluted beyond hope of return?

"Sienna," Finn whispered, as he knelt by her side and stroked her titian hair away from her forehead. "Wake up now. It's okay. We're here." He kissed her lips softly with the gentlest touch.

Sienna's eyes flickered open and for a moment, Mila could see the blue was tinged with silver, edged with dark storm clouds and flashing with lightning. Then Sienna blinked and the clouds cleared as she wrapped her arms around Finn.

He hugged her close, rocking her back and forth. "You're safe now."

Sienna leaned back, her face stricken with fear. "No, none of us are safe. I've seen what they can do, what power they have now. There's only one way to stop this."

CHAPTER 24

Sienna looked up at Finn, tears welling in her eyes. "We have to close the borders. For good this time. We have to shut the gates and stop the worlds bleeding into each other. It's the only way."

Finn reeled back and stood up, pacing the tent. "But then the plague will be trapped here. What if it spreads amongst my people?"

Visions of the creatures she had seen within the shadow-weave filled Sienna's mind, taunting her with the promise of more pain. But now she could see that pain reflected on Finn's face. She had crossed the border thinking that somehow they could find a way to be together, to save his world, and now her only plan was to shut the door and leave him behind in the path of destruction.

"They can stop the plague as surely as they're spreading it. But they won't if it reaches Earthside, and I have to protect my home."

Finn spun round, his eyes blazing with anger, fists clenched. "Your home? What about mine? You leave us all to die from a plague resurrected to destroy *your* people." He shook his head. "But what else would you do? Jari was right, you'll always be Earthsiders and like the rest of your unwanted and forgotten, you will keep pushing us out, denying our right to live."

Sienna wept at his words, tears streaming down her face. "No, Finn. I want to help. I—"

"We don't want it. Your help just makes everything worse." Finn stalked out of the tent into the maelstrom beyond.

"Wait! Please!" Sienna tried to get to her feet but her legs were weak and her body ached from deep inside.

Mila helped her up and as they stood together looking at the empty doorway, Sienna remembered Mila's face as they left Ekon behind at the rim of the pool in Ganvié. This was what her father tried to save her from when he hid her Mapwalker heritage. Love across borders could split a soul apart.

She wanted to run after Finn, fall into his arms, kiss him and stay in that moment forever. Yet every moment they stood here meant Earthside was one step closer to a plague that would shatter her home.

Sienna took a deep breath. "We have to go. Right now."

She turned to the table and pulled her ritual knife from inside her jacket. She held it against the side of her palm where the last cut had barely healed. The blood around it looked almost black and Sienna could see tendrils of shadow that ran deeper through her veins. She was so close to the edge now and part of her wondered what Sir Douglas would have shown her in the room at the top of the mysterious tower. Could she have saved the Borderlands from within? If she became a Shadow Cartographer, could she reshape this side of the world?

"Are you strong enough for this?" Perry's voice was gentle and Sienna knew he understood. His body and soul were battered from this trip, and Mila's, too. It had taken a toll on them all.

"Let's go home." Sienna opened the cut and drew the lines of a map on the wooden table with her blood. Bath Abbey bound by the lines of the river, the canal and the streets of the ancient city. She reached out her hand for her friends and closed her eyes, shutting out the cries of the damned as she traveled back home.

* * *

As the Illuminated Cartographer's pulse slowed, Bridget looked around at the library. On the surface, it was burned to ash, hundreds of years of history charred and blistered beyond recognition. Maps they could no longer travel through, precious tomes they could no longer go to for ancient wisdom, the past now turned to embers.

But as she looked closer, Bridget could see that not all was lost. There were layers of maps under the burnt ones, where the chaos of the Illuminated Cartographer's room had protected what lay beneath. Not all the books were ruined in the fallen shelves and even the globe lay on its side, dented, but not broken.

This was not the end. Not on her watch.

She pulled away from John's hand and her heart almost broke to see the pain in his eyes. He would understand one day but right now, there was no time for debate or argument.

"I have to do this."

John backed away. "Then you must do it alone. You've chosen a path I can't follow." He turned and walked out the door, leaving Bridget in the library alone with the dying Illuminated Cartographer.

She leaned down and whispered in his ear, "I choose this path. For Galileo."

For a moment, she thought she was too late. His eyes remained closed and his skin cooled under her touch.

But then the map fragments that curled around her wrist tightened and more of them began to wind around her limbs until she was pinned beneath the vellum and paper, the lines on them pulsing as if they searched for something in her, something that they could call home.

A sharp piercing pain in her right wrist and then her left.

Bridget screamed in agony as the ink from the maps merged with her blood and the maps transferred themselves from the Illuminated Cartographer over to her own body. They delved deeper into her veins until her heartbeat began to pulse through them.

The pain was still intense but suddenly Bridget could see into the maps themselves, and sense that she could fly into them in a new way. She could travel out through their portals in her mind even though her physical self would remain here, tethered to the library until her own end came.

It was at once terrifying and breathtaking and she desperately wanted to tell John.

But he was gone and she was here alone. Trapped here in the depths of the Abbey, shackled to the maps. The realization struck her. What had she done? Could she undo it?

Bridget began to pull at the maps surrounding her, tugging at their entwined fibers, desperately trying to rip them out of her skin. She sobbed in frustration, blood and ink dripping down her arms as she tried to escape her fate.

* * *

Sienna opened her eyes in the Gallery of Geographical Maps. It was still the same place that they had left from not so long ago, but she felt a deep sense of loss this time. Everything had changed but it wasn't over yet.

Perry and Mila lay at her feet, slowly sitting up as they revived from the vertigo of traveling through the blood map.

Alarms rang through the Ministry, the sharp sound a warning of attack, or perhaps an indication that it had already begun. The smell of burning hung in the air.

The library. The Illuminated Cartographer.

All at once, Sienna understood what Sir Douglas had left

to do while she lay in the shadow-weave. Were they too late?

"Quick, we have to get to the library." Sienna dragged Mila and Perry to their feet and together they hurried down the corridors.

The door to the library was wide open, a scene of devastation within. Her father sat outside, his back against the wall, his head in his hands as he wept.

"Dad?"

John looked up, relief washing over his face. "Sienna, you made it back."

"Are we too late?"

John shook his head. "I don't know. But I can't go in there. I know what she must do but I will lose her forever if she chooses that path."

Sienna frowned at his words. They didn't make any sense.

But as she walked into the library, the pieces suddenly fell into place.

The sound of sobbing came from the corner and behind a pile of burnt maps, Bridget sat next to the body of what had been the Illuminated Cartographer. The maps now wound themselves into Bridget's body even as she tried to scratch them out with bloody fingers, her face puffy with weeping.

"Help me," Bridget begged. "Get them out of my skin. I want to be free. Please."

Perry rushed forward to help, but Sienna grabbed his arm and held him back. She shook her head, resolve strengthening inside.

"There's no time, Bridget. You are the Illuminated Cartographer now. Your blood strengthens the borders. If you reject the maps, we are all lost. Earthside is lost."

Sienna knelt by Bridget's side and placed her hands over the wounds on her wrists where the maps entered her body. "I've seen the plague, and what the Shadow Cartographers can do now. They've bred magic like we have never seen before. We can't win this right now. We need time to regroup, rebuild, and figure this out." Sienna took a deep breath. "Close the borders now, Bridget. Seal them shut and stop the plague from devastating our world."

* * *

Bridget heard Sienna's words as if she was under a swimming pool, the sounds muffled and dense. She felt the young woman's hands on her wounds and the mingling of their blood from a wound on Sienna's palm. She was a powerful Blood Mapwalker, only just beginning to know her powers, but there was a darkness, too. The Shadow had its hooks in her and Bridget knew how good that felt.

But it would not win here today.

For in the mingling of their blood, Bridget saw the camp in the Borderlands, she witnessed the plague rats and Elf's power, the death of Xander and his lion — and Finn's face as he turned his back on love. Just like John as he walked out the library.

This Mapwalker life had taken everything from them both, but they couldn't stop now. Sienna was right. Closing the border was the only choice until the plague burned itself out in the Borderlands and they had the magic on Earthside to stop the Shadow.

From all her study in the annals of the Mapwalkers, Bridget knew that the border had only been closed once before centuries ago. She had read the annals about that occasion once but the details were hazy. There were great risks to both worlds in closing the borders but there was no time to review them now.

Bridget took a deep breath and relaxed into the pile of maps, letting their bulk take her weight. They softened around her in welcome and she sensed the possibilities in her new life.

"I'll do it," she whispered.

Bridget closed her eyes and reached out with her mind through the loops and byways and mountain ranges of the cartographic world. She sensed the line of the border between worlds battered by the plague-infested hordes and on the other side, Earthsiders walked unaware of the danger. Perhaps it was time they knew of what lay beyond. But for now, the Mapwalkers would uphold the ancient pledge — For Galileo.

Bridget poured her blood magic into the border, strengthening the line until it pulsed a deep scarlet, rising up to new heights and thickening to a huge wall as the border slammed shut.

In the far distance, she heard a howl of rage, a thousand thousand tormented souls trapped inside the Shadow, lost in the darkness. There would be a reckoning, but not today.

CHAPTER 25

Two weeks later.

SIENNA LAY ON HER back on the polished wooden floor of her grandfather's flat above the map shop. The sun streamed in through the high windows and lit her skin with the warmth of summer. Bath was blooming, the blossoms lay thick on the trees, birds sung in nearby Victoria Park and tourists strolled the streets with no inkling of what had almost befallen this land.

After such an intense mission, time apart from her friends was strange but necessary. Mila worked on her canal boat, repainting the decorative lines of the winding waterways as her spaniel, Zippy, lay ever watchful by her side.

Perry helped Sienna's father and others from the Ministry repair the damage to the library. They worked around Bridget who was still getting used to being tethered to the maps. She kept trying to walk out the door only to be pulled back into the scrolls. Sienna had caught her weeping more than once since the day she had made her choice and closed the border.

She sighed as she thought of Finn and the last time they had spoken, his rage at her justified, of course, but the pain still lingered. This was her home and she had saved it — but at what cost?

They had no way of knowing what was happening in the Borderlands now. Had the plague decimated the innocent? Had Sir Douglas stopped it with the help of Elf, or had her dark magic turned to creating even worse horrors?

And where was Finn? In the arms of Jari, the warrior woman, or sacrificed at the hands of his father, the Warlord?

Sienna had to get back over there. Somehow, she had to find a way without jeopardizing Earthside. She looked up at the shelves above, her grandfather's journals stacked in neat rows, full of diagrams and his thoughts over a lifetime of mapwalking. She thought of the Nubian woman, the Librarian, a love lost over the border, just like her own. It was time to get to know her grandfather better and perhaps she would find the answers to her own problems in his journals.

As she lay back, she noticed another book on the floor beneath the shelves. Sienna turned over and reached as far as she could underneath the bookcase and pulled it out. She dusted it off and noticed the number on the spine: 24.

The missing journal.

She opened the first page and began to read about something called the Map of the Impossible …

ENJOYED MAP OF PLAGUES?

Thanks for joining Sienna and the Mapwalker team in *Map of Plagues*. If you enjoyed the book, a review would be much appreciated as it helps other readers discover the story.

Get a free copy of the bestselling thriller, *Day of the Vikings*, an ARKANE thriller, when you sign up to join my Reader's Group. You'll also be notified of giveaways, new releases, including the next Mapwalker book, and receive personal updates from behind the scenes of my books.

Click here to get started:

www.JFPenn.com/free

Day of the Vikings, an ARKANE thriller

A ritual murder on a remote island under the shifting skies of the aurora borealis.

A staff of power that can summon Ragnarok, the Viking apocalypse.

When Neo-Viking terrorists invade the British Museum in London to reclaim the staff of Skara Brae, ARKANE agent Dr. Morgan Sierra is trapped in the building along with hostages under mortal threat.

As the slaughter begins, Morgan works alongside psychic Blake Daniel to discern the past of the staff, dating back to islands invaded by the Vikings generations ago.

Can Morgan and Blake uncover the truth before Ragnarok is unleashed, consuming all in its wake?

Day of the Vikings is a fast-paced, supernatural thriller set in London and the islands of Orkney, Lindisfarne and Iona. Set in the present day, it resonates with the history and myth of the Vikings.

If you love an action-packed thriller,
you can get Day of the Vikings for free now:

WWW.JFPENN.COM/FREE

Day of the Vikings features Dr. Morgan Sierra from the ARKANE thrillers, and Blake Daniel from the London Crime Thrillers, but it is also a stand-alone novella that can be read and enjoyed separately.

AUTHOR'S NOTE

Thanks for reading *Map of Plagues*. I hope you enjoyed the adventure. I always like to include an Author's Note in my novels as I love the research process as much as the creative part of writing.

You can find images used in my research on my Pinterest board: www.pinterest.com/jfpenn/map-of-plagues

Bath and finding home

When I wrote the previous book, *Map of Shadows*, we had just moved to Bath in the South West of England. I found it difficult at first and struggled with a place that seemed almost too perfect, a heritage city of Roman and Georgian grandeur as well as natural beauty. I'm a happy person but as a fan of Stephen King's books, I can't help but think that everywhere has a dark side! After all, Mary Shelley wrote most of *Frankenstein* here in Bath, so it definitely has a shadow element.

Writing *Map of Shadows* helped me understand Bath in a deeper way and I found my dark side again, then as I wrote the first draft of *Map of Plagues* we bought a house here. In a reflection of my own journey, this book shows Sienna settling on her own home in Bath and Mila questioning where her true place might lie.

At the same time, I also started a new podcast, *Books and Travel*, which is all about my search for a home and the places I have traveled along the way, as well as interviews with other authors about the places that inspire their stories. Check it out on your favorite podcast app or at www.BooksAndTravel.page.

Other places that inspired the story

The prologue describes a plague pit behind the Tower of London near the Royal Mint. This is a real site as documented on the London Plague Pits Map and excavations date the bones to 1348–1350.

Like many bibliophiles, the ancient Library of Alexandria is one of those places that I long to visit. I couldn't help but write it in. The Scryers are influenced by *The Dark Crystal* film, which I saw when I was seven years old and remains one of my recurrent nightmares. My little brother used to chase me with his hands like claws shouting, "I'll suck the life out of you." I hadn't thought of it for years but a new film, *The Dark Crystal: Age of Resistance*, is being released in 2019, and I happened to see a trailer and those nightmares emerged once more.

Ganvié Island is a real village built on Lake Nokoué in Benin but, as with Aleppo, I had it straddle the border between worlds. I wanted Mila to discover a glimpse of her possible ancestry and maybe she will even return to Ekon in another story …

The city under the waves was based on an underwater city found in the Gulf of Cambay in India, thought to be from 9000 BCE, which would make it the oldest civilization on earth. I recently narrated my own audiobook of *The Dark Queen* short story and found myself immersed in underwater archaeology once more.

Aetofolia, the eagle's nest, is based on Meteora, a Greek monastery perched on the side of the cliff, and also the landscape of the Zhangjiajie National Forest Park in China which was used as the inspiration for Pandora in *Avatar*.

Themes

I wrote the previous book, *Map of Shadows* after the Brexit vote in the UK. The theme of borders and being denied access runs through that story.

In a similar way, the news since has been filled with stories of refugees from war, climate change or those just searching for a new life with more opportunities. As countries build walls and strengthen borders, many refugees are turned away and it's not too much of a stretch to think of them ending up in the Borderlands. Perhaps there is an answer in *Map of the Impossible*?

ACKNOWLEDGMENTS

Thanks to Jen Blood, for continuing to make me laugh during edits. Thanks to Wendy Janes for proofreading, and to my Pennfriends for useful advanced reader comments.

Thanks to Jane Dixon Smith at JDSmith-Design.com for the great cover design and print formatting.

MORE BOOKS BY J.F.PENN

Thanks for joining Sienna and the
Mapwalker team in *Map of Plagues*.

Sign up at www.JFPenn.com/free to be notified of the next
book in the series and receive my monthly updates and
giveaways.

* * *

Mapwalker Dark Fantasy Thrillers

Map of Shadows #1
Map of Plagues #2
Map of the Impossible #3 (available 2020)

If you like **supernatural thrillers**, check out the **ARKANE**
series as Morgan Sierra and Jake Timber solve supernatural
mysteries around the world.

Stone of Fire #1
Crypt of Bone #2
Ark of Blood #3
One Day In Budapest #4
Day of the Vikings #5
Gates of Hell #6
One Day in New York #7
Destroyer of Worlds #8
End of Days #9
Valley of Dry Bones #10

* * *

If you like **crime thrillers with an edge of the supernatural**, join Detective Jamie Brooke and museum researcher Blake Daniel, in the London crime thriller trilogy:

Desecration #1
Delirium #2
Deviance #3

* * *

For more **dark fantasy,** check out:

Risen Gods
The Dark Queen
A Thousand Fiendish Angels:
Short stories based on Dante's Inferno

More books coming soon.

You can sign up to be notified of new releases, giveaways and pre-release specials - plus, get a free book!

www.JFPenn.com/free

If you loved the book and have a moment to spare, I would really appreciate a short review on the page where you bought the book. Your help in spreading the word is gratefully appreciated and reviews make a huge difference to helping new readers find the series.

Thank you!

ABOUT THE AUTHOR

J.F.Penn is the Award-nominated, New York Times and USA Today bestselling author of the ARKANE supernatural thrillers, London Crime Thrillers, and the Mapwalker dark fantasy series, as well as other standalone stories.

Her books weave together ancient artifacts, relics of power, international locations and adventure with an edge of the supernatural. Joanna lives in Bath, England and enjoys a nice G&T.

You can follow Joanna's travels on Instagram @jfpennauthor and also on her podcast at BooksAndTravel.page.

* * *

You can sign up for a free thriller, Day of the Vikings, and updates from behind the scenes, research, and giveaways at:

WWW.JFPENN.COM/FREE

***

Connect at:
www.JFPenn.com
joanna@JFPenn.com
www.Facebook.com/JFPennAuthor
www.Instagram.com/JFPennAuthor
www.Twitter.com/JFPennWriter

* * *

For writers:

Joanna's site, www.TheCreativePenn.com, helps people write, publish and market their books through articles, audio, video and online courses.

She writes non-fiction for authors under Joanna Penn and has an award-nominated podcast for writers, The Creative Penn Podcast.

www.ingramcontent.com/pod-product-compliance
Lightning Source LLC
Chambersburg PA
CBHW030624190726
48286CB00008B/2392